Harold and Maude

A Play in Two Acts

by Colin Higgins

A SAMUEL FRENCH ACTING EDITION

SAMUEL FRENCH

FOUNDED 1830

SAMUELFRENCH.COM

CHARACTERS
(in order of appearance)

HAROLD
MRS. CHASEN
MAID
DR. MATTHEWS
MAUDE
PRIEST
GARDENER
CHIEF GARDENER
SYLVIE GAZEL
INSPECTOR BERNARD
SERGEANT DOPPEL
NANCY MERSCH
SUNSHINE DORE

REMOVAL MEN

HAROLD AND MAUDE

ACT I

Scene 1

PLACE: *A record drops down on a phonograph and we hear the beginnings of Tchaikovsky's "Pathetique." After a few moments, the curtain rises.*

HAROLD'S HOUSE.

The CHASEN living room is that of an upper middle-class home, tastefully furnished but with an air of understated wealth. HAROLD CHASEN, a neatly dressed boy of nineteen is strung up by the neck and hanging from the chandelier. HE is not moving. In fact, HE appears to be dead. The music plays on. After a few moments, we hear voices approaching and MRS. CHASEN, HAROLD's mother, opens the living room door. An elegantly dressed lady with an unflappable manner, SHE stands in the doorway and talks to the new maid, MARIE.

MRS. CHASEN. The liquor is usually kept in the little cabinet there and the glasses are in the sideboard. The ice, of course, you bring in from the kitchen. I don't think you'll have any trouble but if there are any difficulties, just ask.

(*THEY walk to the couch, not noticing HAROLD hanging Upstage behind them.*)

Now, I think, Marie, we will have the hors d'oeuvres in here. The cook has prepared those delightful little shrimp savories that are so tasty when served hot . . . Oh, that music . . . (*SHE goes to the phonograph to turn it off.*) I think if you bring them in on the trolley with the large silver cover they'll keep warm. What do you think?

(*MARIE turns round to answer and sees HAROLD. SHE screams.*)

MARIE. Ahhhhhhh!!

(*MRS. CHASEN switches off the music. SHE glances over at MARIE.*)

MRS. CHASEN. I beg your pardon?

(*MARIE is wildly gesturing with one hand while the other is covering her horror-stricken mouth.*)

MARIE. Ahhh . . . Ahhhh . . .

(*MRS. CHASEN looks Upstage to where MARIE is pointing and sees the hanging body of her son. SHE takes a deep, exasperated breath.*)

MRS. CHASEN. Oh, no! Harold, really! Not in front of the new maid. (*SHE turns to the white-faced MARIE.*) I'm sorry, Marie . . . Harold has absolutely no sense of timing. You'd think that . . . (*SHE sees the clock.*) Oh, goodness, that clock can't be right. Is it? The doctor will be here any minute. Well, I've explained the drinks and the hors d'oeuvres, and I don't think the dinner will be any problem. Do you have any questions?

(*MARIE is still staring at the hanging body and is totally mystified at MRS. CHASEN's apparent disinterest. SHE tries to speak.*)

MARIE. But . . . but . . .
MRS. CHASEN. What? (*SHE looks over at HAROLD and shakes her head.*) Oh, yes. Isn't that typical? I have a hundred-and-one things to worry about and he hasn't even dressed for dinner! (*SHE goes Upstage and stands under the chandelier.*) Harold?

(*no response*)

Harold! This is your mother speaking!

(*HAROLD cocks his head and opens his eyes. HE looks down at his mother.*)

Come down from there immediately.

(*HAROLD pauses for a moment while HE thinks it over. Then HE resignedly pulls a little string attached to the rope and with a great whirring of machinery overhead, HE is slowly lowered to the floor. MRS. CHASEN watches him descend.*)

Look at those socks! How many times have I told you one does not wear brown socks with black shoes? Really, Harold, sometimes I feel I'm a voice crying in the wilderness. Have you any idea of the time?

(*The bell rings.*)

Here is Doctor Matthews, and you . . . you're not even wearing a tie.

(*HAROLD removes the noose from around his neck.*)

Marie . . .

(*MARIE has been standing, dazed and dumbfounded, ever since SHE first saw HAROLD. MRS. CHASEN has to call her again to get her attention.*)

Marie? What's the matter, dear? You're looking a little pale.
MARIE. Oh, nothing.

(*The doorbell rings again.*)

MRS. CHASEN. Well, that's the doorbell.
MARIE. (*finally snapping out of it*) Oh, yes. Excuse me. (*SHE exits.*)
MRS. CHASEN. Now listen, Harold. Doctor Matthews, at my request, has taken the time to come here tonight to meet you. Please take advantage of it. Talk with him. Meet with him. He is eminently qualified and I think once you begin co-operating you will find him very helpful. God knows, he was absolutely marvelous with me.

(*MARIE ushers in DOCTOR MATTHEWS, a tall, silver-haired man with an unctious manner. SHE takes his coat and exits Upstage as MRS. CHASEN comes over to greet him.*)

Doctor, so nice to see you. How have you been?
   DOCTOR. Very well, thanks. And you, Helen?
   MRS. CHASEN. Oh, fine. Just fine. Doctor, I'd like you to meet my son, Harold. Harold, this is Doctor Matthews.
   DOCTOR. Hello there. I've heard a lot about you.

(*HAROLD mutters a shy hello and shakes the DOCTOR's hand. There is a slight pause as the DOCTOR looks at the noose and hanging harness HAROLD is carrying. MRS. CHASEN breaks the silence.*)

   MRS. CHASEN. Well now, Harold. Why don't you take your . . . *things* upstairs and get ready for dinner? We'll wait for you down here. But do hurry up.

(*HAROLD takes a note from the table and exits. MRS. CHASEN and the DOCTOR go over to the couch.*)

Please sit down, Doctor. I'm so glad you could come. I sometimes wonder if I'm strong enough to raise a boy all on my own.

(*MARIE enters.*)

What would you like to drink? Scotch?
   DOCTOR. Yes, that would be fine.
   MRS. CHASEN. One Scotch, Marie, and a glass of white wine.

MARIE. Yes, Madam. (*SHE exits.*)

MRS. CHASEN. Well, you know how difficult it was after Charles' death. The business to keep going . . . this house . . . my hospital charity. It has not been easy.

DOCTOR. No.

MRS. CHASEN. Not that it was any sleigh ride while Charles was alive. He could be just as trying as Harold. Well, I told you about our wedding. What other bride would wait 25 minutes at the altar while her husband-to-be was at home in the bath thoroughly absorbed in the workings of a mechanical duck? Oh, no, Doctor, it has not been easy.

(*MARIE enters with the drinks and serves them. SHE exits.*)

Thank you, Marie. Oh, well, enough about the past. What I'm worried about is Harold. He needs you, Doctor. I hope you can help him. I don't seem to be reaching him any more. Not that he was ever really a talkative boy. Intelligent, yes. And very creative. You should have a look at the things in his room. But talkative, no. Well, you saw yourself.

DOCTOR. He seemed a little . . .

MRS. CHASEN. He hardly says two words to strangers. I've tried to teach him the social graces. I sent him to dancing school when he was eleven. But nothing took. At parties, he'll just wander off and sit by himself. That can be very trying, as you can imagine – particularly when it's his own party.

(*MARIE enters with the hors d'oeuvres trolley and wheels it over to the couch.*)

DOCTOR. Yes. Well, perhaps after dinner he and I can sit down and talk. Maybe even set up some appointments in the office.

MRS. CHASEN. That would be marvellous – and a great load off my mind. You see, Doctor, this is very difficult for a mother to say – but lately sometimes I look at him and think he's completely lost his head.

(*MARIE takes the large silver cover off the plate of hors d'oeuvres revealing HAROLD's decapitated head lying à la John the Baptist amongst the parsley.*

MARIE drops the cover and screams. MRS. CHASEN and the DOCTOR look over just as a headless HAROLD [a double] comes through the door and nonchalantly takes the seat by the couch. MRS. CHASEN and the DOCTOR seem more confused than horrified, but the effect is not lost on MARIE. With bulging eyes and gasping breath, SHE collapses in a dead faint on the floor.)

BLACKOUT

ACT I

Scene 2

PLACE: *THE PSYCHIATRIST's AREA.*

The Lights Come Up immediately in the DOCTOR's office to find the real HAROLD lying on the psychiatrist's couch with the DOCTOR sitting in a chair beside him.

DOCTOR. Tell me, Harold, how many of these . . . eh, suicides have you performed?

HAROLD. (*after a long thoughtful pause*) An accurate number would be difficult to gauge.

DOCTOR. And why is that?

HAROLD. Well, I'm not sure if I should count the first time since that wasn't really planned, and then, of course, there was the time the gas oven exploded before my mother even got home from her party. Then there's those in the planning stages, those that were abandoned, the question of maiming . . .

DOCTOR. (*interrupting*) Just give me a rough estimate.

HAROLD. (*after a pause*) I'd say fifteen.

DOCTOR. Fifteen.

HAROLD. That's a rough estimate.

DOCTOR. And were they all done for your mother's benefit?

HAROLD. (*after another pause*) I don't think I'd say . . . "benefit".

DOCTOR. No, I suppose not. But they were all designed to elicit a particular response from your mother, isn't that so? For example, she told me she was reduced to hysterics the day you shot your head off with a shotgun.

HAROLD. Yes, that one went very well. It's not an easy stunt to do, you know. The fake charge sometimes goes off before the spring shoots out the blood.

DOCTOR. But you were satisfied with your mother's reaction?

HAROLD. (*nodding agreement*) 'Course that was one of the first. It was a lot easier then.

DOCTOR. How do you mean?

HAROLD. Well, take the hanging the other night. I worked for three days on that and I don't think she even saw the suicide note.

DOCTOR. What did it say?

HAROLD. That one said: "This is the end – farewell". I'm making them shorter.

DOCTOR. Let's talk about your mother. How do you feel about her?

HAROLD. Ah, . . .

(*Before HAROLD can answer, the LIGHTS GO OUT on the psychiatrist's area and COME UP immediately on MRS. CHASEN at home. SHE is talking on the phone to her hairdresser while going through her daily massage.*)

MRS. CHASEN. No, no, Betty. Lydia Fergusson. I sent her to you for a blue rinse. Well, I invited Lydia's daughter Alice over to meet Harold . . . yes, a rather pudgy little thing – takes after Lydia in that respect. We went down to the tennis court and what do we find but Harold floating face down in the pool with a knife oozing blood stuck in the middle of his back . . . Of course, the poor girl screamed. Screamed and fled. I doubt if the Fergussons will ever speak to me again. I don't know what to do, Betty, really I don't . . . He's been going to Doctor Matthews but I've seen very little result. What he needs is responsibility. Settle down and get married but where am I going to find him a bride? . . . What's that? . . . The computer dating service. What an excellent idea! . . . You say they guarantee at least three girls. Well, surely we can find one who is suitable. I'll call them immediately . . . What's that . . . Mario? Well, I'm sorry. You'll just have to tell him to change it to Tuesday. I'm a mother whose son needs her help. I can't be held down to a pedicure.

(*The LIGHTS GO OFF on MRS. CHASEN and COME UP on the psychiatrist's area. The DOCTOR and HAROLD break their freeze.*)

DOCTOR. I see. Now let's talk about your father. What do you remember about him?

HAROLD. Nothing really . . . (*pause*) I have some pictures of him.

DOCTOR. (*prompting*) Yes . . .

HAROLD. He was always smiling.

DOCTOR. You would have liked to know him, then?

HAROLD. Uh huh. I would have liked to talk to him.

DOCTOR. What about?

HAROLD. Oh, different things. Mother said he was very mechanical. I would have showed him the stuff in my room.

DOCTOR. What stuff is that?

HAROLD. You know, all my equipment—my daggers, my skeleton, my electric chair. I think he would have liked it.

DOCTOR. Very interesting. Tell me, Harold, what do you think of young ladies?

HAROLD. I like them.

DOCTOR. Do you have any girlfriends?

HAROLD. No. Not really.

DOCTOR. Why not?

HAROLD. I don't think they like me.

DOCTOR. And why is that?

HAROLD. (*He thinks of one reason.*) In dancing school, I used to tread on their toes.

DOCTOR. (*Heaving a sigh, HE changes the subject.*) Well . . . Let's talk a little about boarding school. Were you happy there?

HAROLD. Oh, yes.

DOCTOR. You liked your teachers?

HAROLD. Yes.

DOCTOR. Your classmates?

HAROLD. Yes.

DOCTOR. Your studies?

HAROLD. Yes.

DOCTOR. Then why did you leave?

HAROLD. I burned down the chemistry building . . . (*pause*) After that they decided I'd better take my exams by mail.

DOCTOR. So you stayed home?

HAROLD. I didn't mind.

DOCTOR. But don't you ever go out?

HAROLD. Oh, yes. I go to junkyards and demolitions.

DOCTOR. I see. But what is it you do for fun?

HAROLD. That's fun.

DOCTOR. I'm sure it is. But apart from that what do you do for relaxation?

HAROLD. (*thinking*) You mean, when I'm not in my room working on one of my . . .

DOCTOR. (*interrupting*) Yes. Yes.

HAROLD. (*pause*) I go to funerals.

BLACKOUT

ACT I

Scene 3

Place: *INSIDE A CHURCH.*

An organ is softly playing funereal music as the set changes to the inside of a church. HAROLD walks down the center aisle to where the coffin is standing, pauses to look at it, and then sits in one of the empty pews on the right. HE waits. His eye catches the picnic basket on the pew beside him and HE looks around for its owner. Suddenly, HE hears a movement under the seat behind him and as HE turns around, MAUDE, a charming old lady, pops up and smiles at him.

MAUDE. Pardon me, do you see any nuts?
HAROLD. What?
MAUDE. Nuts. (*SHE stands up and looks around his feet.*) No, I think I've got them all. (*offering the bag*) Here, would you like one?
HAROLD. No, thanks.
MAUDE. Go ahead. They're very nutritious.
HAROLD. No, really.
MAUDE. Okay, maybe later. Oh, here's another. (*SHE picks it up and walks around to HAROLD's pew.*) Well, I hope that's the lot. I just pulled the bag out of my basket

16

and – whoosh! – they fell all over the floor. I must be getting clumsy in my old age. (*SHE sits down beside HAROLD with the basket beside her. HE is a little nervous but SHE smiles at him warmly as SHE munches on a couple of nuts.*) Did you know him?

HAROLD. Who?

MAUDE. (*gesturing at the casket*) The deceased.

HAROLD. Ah, no.

MAUDE. Me, neither. I hear he was 80 years old. Good time to move on, don't you think?

HAROLD. I don't know.

MAUDE. Well, I mean 75 is too early and at 85 you're just marking time and you may as well look over the horizon. Like an orange?

HAROLD. No, thank you.

MAUDE. You don't eat much, do you?

HAROLD. Well, I . . . (*thinking quickly*) I don't want to spoil my lunch. In fact . . . (*HE glances at his watch.*)

MAUDE. You go to funerals often?

HAROLD. Well, ah . . .

MAUDE. Oh, yes, so do I. They're such fun, aren't they? It's all change. All revolving. Burials and births. The end to the beginning, the beginning to the end. The great circle of life . . . What's your name?

HAROLD. Harold. Harold Chasen.

MAUDE. I'm the Countess Mathilda Chardin, but you may call me Maude.

HAROLD. Nice to meet you. Well . . . (looking at his watch again)

MAUDE. Just look around you, Harold. Isn't this astounding? Gloom and black, unsmiling saints, and . . . (*points*) all those crucifixes – why do you suppose they go on about that? You'd think no one ever read the end of the story.

(*A shy timorous little PRIEST enters, sees MAUDE eating, and rushes over, horrified. His name is FATHER FINNEGAN.*)

PRIEST. Madam! Madam, what are you doing?

MAUDE. Oh, hello, Reverend. We're waiting for the service. Are you going to preside?

PRIEST. Yes, but, Madam, you can't eat in here. It's . . . it's not allowed.

MAUDE. Oh, how silly. This is the House of God, isn't it?

PRIEST. Yes, but . . .

MAUDE. And He wants us to be happy, doesn't he?

PRIEST. Yes, but . . .

MAUDE. Well, then—what's the problem?

PRIEST. But, Madam, this is a funeral.

MAUDE. Ah, yes, I was just discussing that with Harold. Why do you think there's this mania for black? I mean, no one sends black flowers, do they? Black flowers are dead flowers and who would send dead flowers to a funeral? (*SHE laughs.*) Isn't that absurd?

HAROLD. (*deciding HE's had enough*) Excuse me, I think I'd better be going.

MAUDE. Lunch?

HAROLD. Eh, yes.

MAUDE. Well, eat well, Harold. I hope we meet again real soon.

(*HAROLD nods and exits. The LIGHTS BEGIN TO DIM.*)

PRIEST. Now, Madam, I must talk to you about . . .

MAUDE. Oh, good. I'd love a little chat too. Actually there are several things I've been meaning to bring to your attention. Those saints, for example. Look at them. Not a smile in the groups. How silly. I mean a saint should be happy, don't you think? An unhappy saint is a contradiction in terms.

PRIEST. Well, you may have a point, Madam . . .

MAUDE. Maude.

PRIEST. But about those nuts . . .

MAUDE. Oh, I'm sorry. I don't think I have any more. How about an orange? (*SHE begins to look for one.*)

PRIEST. No, thank you. I have a service in five minutes and . . .

MAUDE. Oh, that's lots of time. Come on with me. I've always wanted to ask why is it you have a lock on the poor box?

PRIEST. We've always had a lock on the poor box.

MAUDE. (*giving him a lock from her basket*) Not any more. (*SHE walks off. The PRIEST holds the lock and then follows her in amazement.*)

BLACKOUT

ACT I

Scene 4

PLACE: *HAROLD'S HOUSE.*

MRS. CHASEN comes into the living room with a sheaf of papers. SHE sees HAROLD in the doorway and motions for HIM to come over.

MRS. CHASEN. I have here, Harold, the forms sent out by the National Computer Dating Service. It seems to me that this is a marvellous step in finding you a prospective wife.

HAROLD. Wife?

MRS. CHASEN. Yes, dear. I think it is time you got married.

HAROLD. But . . .

MRS. CHASEN. Harold, please. There is a lot of work for us here to do and I have to be at the hairdresser's at three. (*SHE goes to her desk and sits.*)

HAROLD. But I don't want to get married.

MRS. CHASEN. (*indulgently*) I'm sure everyone has felt that way one time or another. But we must face realities. It's called growing up. (*SHE looks through papers.*) The Computer Dating Service offers you at least three dates on the initial investment. They say they screen out the fat and ugly, so it's obviously a firm of high standards. They seem certain they can find you at least one girl who is compatible. Now, please, dear, sit down.

(*HAROLD gives up protesting and sits down. MRS. CHASEN takes out the first questionnaire.*)

MRS. CHASEN. Here is the personality interview which you are to fill out and return. There are fifty questions with five possibilities to check: Absolutely yes – Yes – Not sure – No – and, Absolutely no. Are you ready, Harold?

(*HAROLD stares at his mother with mournful eyes. MRS. CHASEN takes this as agreement.*)

The first question is: Do you constantly wash your hands? Constantly? No. Wouldn't you agree, Harold? Perhaps even an "absolutely no". (*SHE marks the paper—as SHE continues to do throughout the scene.*) Number two: Do you enjoy spending a lot of time by yourself? Well, that's easy, isn't it? Absolutely yes. Three. Should sex education be taught outside the home? I would say no, wouldn't you, Harold. Should women run for President of the United States? I don't see why not. Absolutely yes. Do you often invite friends to your home? No, you never do, Harold. Absolutely no. Do you often get the feeling that perhaps life isn't worth living? Hmmm . . . (*SHE pauses thoughtfully and glances up.*) What would you say, Harold?

(*HAROLD is taken unawares.*)

HAROLD. Huh?
MRS. CHASEN. You think yes or no?

(*HAROLD begins to say something but SHE cuts him off.*)

Well, let's put down—not sure. Seven: Do you prefer a sunrise more than a sunset? No. I wouldn't say that. Is the subject of sex being over-exploited by our mass media? That would have to be "yes", wouldn't it? Do judges favor some lawyers? Yes, I suppose they do.

(*As MRS. CHASEN continues, HAROLD nonchalantly reaches inside his coat and brings out a stick of dynamite. HE fondles it lovingly and smoothes out the wick.*)

Do you sometimes have headaches or backaches after a difficult day? Yes, I do indeed. Do you go to sleep easily? I'd say no. Is it difficult for you to accept criticism? No, not at all.

(*HAROLD reaches down into the side of his boot and takes out another stick of dynamite. HE fondles it like the first.*)

Do you believe in capital punishment for murder? Oh, yes. Do you believe churches have a strong influence to upgrade the general morality? Yes, again. In your opinion are social affairs usually a waste of time? Heavens no!

(*HAROLD reaches down into his other boot and takes out a third stick of dynamite. MRS. CHASEN continues, oblivious to all of this.*)

Can God influence our lives? Yes. Absolutely yes. Have you ever crossed the street to avoid meeting someone? Well, I'm sure you have, haven't you, dear? (*SHE glances up at him.*) Eh? Yes, I'm sure you have . . . (*SHE marks the question and turns the page while HAROLD puts a thick rubber band around the three sticks of dynamite and twists their fuses together.*) Eighteen: Did you enjoy life as a child? Oh, yes. You were a wonderful baby, Harold. Does your personal religion or philosophy include a life after death? Oh, yes, indeed. That's absolutely.

(*HAROLD has struck a match and is lighting the dynamite.*)

Do you have ups and downs without obvious reasons?

You do, don't you, dear? Do you remember jokes and take pleasure in relating them to others? . . .

(*HAROLD stands up with the rapidly burning dynamite and walks toward his mother.*)

No, you don't, do you, dear? Do you think the sexual revolution . . . (*SHE looks up and sighs.*) Harold, would you *please* sit down?

(*HAROLD walks past her to the closet, opens the door and steps inside. As soon as HE closes the door, a mighty explosion shakes the stage, blasting the door off its hinges and sending billows of smoke out into the room. MRS. CHASEN watches the smoke drift away with the rising impatience of a set-upon schoolteacher.*)

Harold, I'm waiting . . . (*flatly*) The question is: Do you think the sexual revolution has gone too far?

BLACKOUT

ACT I

Scene 5

PLACE: *A LARGE CEMETERY.*

The sound of birds and the tolling of a church bell as the LIGHTS COME UP to reveal a sunny cemetery.

Three or four MOURNERS are far Upstage Left attending a burial that is taking place just Offstage.

HAROLD stands apart from them, more Downstage but with his back to the audience. HE and the OTHERS are listening to a PRIEST read out the final prayers and from the sound of his timorous voice we recognize him to be the same little PRIEST we met earlier.

After a few moments, MAUDE enters Downstage Right, carrying a shovel. SHE looks about for a moment, then finding the right spot SHE sticks the shovel into the dirt and exits. The PRIEST finishes the prayers and the Upstage MOURNERS begin to file Off. HAROLD is about to follow when MAUDE enters, pushing a wheelbarrow containing a small tree. SHE stops and looks about for someone to help her.

MAUDE. Eh, excuse me, but . . . Harold? Is that you? Oh, what a delight it is to bump into you again. How have you been?

HAROLD. (*doesn't really want to talk*) Oh, fine. I'm . . . (*HE points Off.*)

MAUDE. Oh, whose funeral is that?

HAROLD. I don't know.

MAUDE. Hmmm. I'm sorry I'm missing it. (*looking Off*) And isn't that the nice little priest, Father Finnegan, we were talking to in church yesterday?

HAROLD. Yes.

MAUDE. Oh, I'll have to drop over and say hello. But

first, Harold, I need your help. Could you come over here for a minute?

(*THEY walk over to the wheelbarrow.*)

HAROLD. What are you doing?
MAUDE. I want to plant this tree.
HAROLD. You mean here?
MAUDE. Yes, look at it, the poor thing. I was just passing by City Hall this morning and there it was — stuck in a cement pot suffocating with all that smog and automobile fumes. So I decided right then to rescue it and replant it where it had some chance for life.
HAROLD. You mean you just took it?
MAUDE. That's right.
HAROLD. But it's public **property.**
MAUDE. Exactly. Look at those little leaves. They're turning brown. People can live with smog, but trees — it gives them asthma. Pick it up, Harold, and I'll hold the barrow steady.
HAROLD. (*still amazed*) Did anyone see you?
MAUDE. I don't know. But I didn't do it to be seen or to be praised. I just felt it was my duty. Go ahead, Harold. Hold it straight. I don't want to upset its circulation.

(*HAROLD lifts the tree and holds it in his arms. MAUDE moves the barrow. A GARDENER enters.*)

GARDENER. Lady, that's my wheelbarrow.
MAUDE. Oh, is it? Well, thank you. I don't think we'll need it any more. Come on over here, Harold.
GARDENER. Wait a minute, lady. What do you think you're doing?

MAUDE. I'm going to dig a hole and . . .

GARDENER. But you can't do that. This is a cemetery.

MAUDE. Oh, I'm not going to bury anything. I'm just going to plant this tree. You explain it to him, Harold.

GARDENER. Wait a minute. Do you have a permit? Did you contact the office?

MAUDE. How could I? I only decided to do it this morning.

GARDENER. Well, listen, lady, you can't just walk in here and start digging holes.

MAUDE. I'm not digging holes. I'm planting a tree. It will look very nice here – once it regains its health. You'll like it.

GARDENER. It's not up to me, lady.

MAUDE. All right. Who is it I should speak to? How about Father Finnegan? I'm sure he'll understand. (*SHE calls Offstage to the little PRIEST.*) Father Finnegan! Yoo-hoo. (*SHE waves. Apparently HE sees her and turns away.*) Hmmm, I don't think he recognized me. (*SHE cries out even louder.*) Father Finnegan! (*And then puts her fingers in her mouth and lets out with an ear-splitting whistle. SHE smiles.*) That did it. Here he comes.

PRIEST. (*entering, a little perturbed*) Madam, you must not do that. I'm in the midst of a service.

MAUDE. I know that, Father, and I wouldn't interrupt if this wasn't a matter of life and death.

PRIEST. Oh? . . . Whose?

MAUDE. This little tree's.

PRIEST. What was that?

GARDENER. All I know is my boss ain't going to allow no digging of no holes.

MAUDE. Allow it? Who does he think he is? Nature?

GARDENER. Look, Father, you'd better tell these two

to take this stuff out of here or I'm going to have to report them.

MAUDE. How can you ask him to do that? This man is a servant of God. He has pledged his life to charity and compassion. And you think that he's going to turn his back on this little tree? Tell him, Father.

PRIEST. (*confused*) Well, I . . . eh.

MAUDE. Of course not. Bring the tree over here, Harold.

GARDENER. Okay, I warned you, lady. Now I'm going to get my boss. And next time you can just leave my wheelbarrow alone! (*HE exits angrily, taking the wheelbarrow with him. HAROLD is still holding the tree and is anxious to get out of this whole affair.*)

MAUDE. Next time? Next time I certainly won't come *here*. I mean there are other places.

PRIEST. Well, perhaps you should take this somewhere else. After all, you have no permission to dig here and if the head gardener says that you'll have to go, I don't see how I can stop him.

MAUDE. Oh, Father, you're not against us, too?

HAROLD. (*speaking up*) As a matter of fact, I don't think that . . .

MAUDE. Now, Harold, I'm not accusing him. (*to the PRIEST*) I'm sure you have your reasons, Father.

PRIEST. Well, I . . . I . . .

(*The GARDENER enters with his Boss, a large, no-nonsense man.*)

BOSS. Say, what's all this I hear about you people wanting to plant a tree?

GARDENER. That's her. She and the kid.

MAUDE. Save your breath, gentlemen. I see your attitude and I've changed my mind. This is not a friendly atmosphere for an invalid. We are going elsewhere – to the forest.

HAROLD. The what?

MAUDE. Come along, Harold. Enough has been said. Let us leave these men with their conscience. (*SHE picks up the shovel and grandly walks out. HAROLD still holding the tree, is left with no recourse but to follow. The GARDENER looks Off as THEY depart while the BOSS turns to the PRIEST.*)

BOSS. I understand she's a friend of yours, Father?

PRIEST. Well . . . an acquaintance. We met yesterday for the first time . . . A very original talker.

BOSS. Well, you better tell her if she gets any more original ideas like that one she'd better stay away from here. I mean we got laws against that kind of thing.

PRIEST. Yes . . . I quite agree with you. Well . . . I think I'd better be getting back.

(*The PRIEST is about to return Upstage when the GARDENER, who has been looking at the departed HAROLD and MAUDE, cries out:*)

GARDENER. Hey, Father, isn't that your car they're getting into?

(*The PRIEST looks off to where HE is pointing. HE opens his mouth in surprise as we hear the sound of a car start up and drive away.*)

PRIEST. (*mystified*) Yes. That's my car.

BLACKOUT

ACT I

Scene 6

Place: *MAUDE'S HOUSE.*

*MAUDE enters and walks to the front of her house
followed by HAROLD, carrying the tree. SHE has
been explaining to HAROLD how SHE is able to
drive off in any car due to the collection of keys SHE
carries in her hand.*

Maude. Oh, Big Sweeney was a marvellous person,
very gifted. He studied Zen Buddhism in the penitentiary
and when he was released took off immediately for Tibet
. . . Just bring the tree over here, Harold . . . But before
he left he gave me his collection of keys. Of course, I've
had to make some additions for the newer models but not
as many as you might think. Once you have your basic
set, it's then only a question of variation.

Harold. Do you mean with that ring of keys you get
into any car you like and just drive off?

Maude. Not *any* car. I like to keep a variety. Here, this
is fine.

(HAROLD puts down the tree.)

Oh, thank you, Harold. We'll take it out to the forest first
thing in the morning.

29

HAROLD. Well, I don't think I can . . .

MAUDE. (*laughing*) I didn't mean we'd walk. Of course, we're going to have to find ourselves a truck.

HAROLD. A truck? You mean, you're just going to take one?

MAUDE. That's right.

HAROLD. But . . . (*gesturing Off*) . . . you've got the priest's car and now you're going to take another . . . I . . . what about the owners?

MAUDE. Oh, what owners, Harold? None of us really owns anything. We come on the earth with nothing and we go out with nothing, so isn't ownership a little absurd?

HAROLD. Maybe, but I still think you're upsetting people, and I'm not sure if that's right.

MAUDE. Well, if some people get upset because they feel they have a hold on some things then I'm merely acting as a gentle reminder. Here today, gone tomorrow, so don't get attached to *things*. Now with that in mind, I'm not against collecting stuff. Come on in, Harold. I've collected quite a lot of stuff in my time. (*MAUDE opens the door and THEY both walk into the living room. It is full of eccentric objects and furniture: a Persian rug, an ivory Buddha, Japanese screens, expensive paintings, a large wooden sculpture, ferns, a birdbath, and to top it all off a live seal is sitting on the piano stool. HAROLD is amazed.*) It's all memorabilia, but incidental, not integral, if you know what I mean.

HAROLD. It's very impressive.

MAUDE. (*pointing*) Oh, look.

(*HAROLD looks to where SHE is pointing and sees the seal sitting by the window. MAUDE walks excitedly over and, ignoring the seal, sticks her head out the window.*)

The birds! They're waiting for lunch. (*SHE takes some bird seed and sprinkles it into a catapult.*) Aren't they gorgeous? They're the only wildlife I see anymore. (*SHE pulls the catapult and bird seed is sprayed into the back yard.*) Ah, me. Free as a bird. (*turning to HAROLD*) You know, at one time I used to break into pet shops and liberate the canaries, but I gave it up as an idea way before its time. (*SHE absently pats the seal on the head.*) The zoos are full, the prisons are overflowing. Dear me, how the world so dearly loves a cage.

HAROLD. Isn't that a seal?

MAUDE. Yes. That's Mister Murgatroyd. He's going to be visiting for a few days. Say hello to Harold, dear.

(*The seal barks.*)

What's that? You want to take a bath? But you just had a bath this morning. Oh, you want another. All right. Excuse me, Harold. I won't be a minute. Come on, Mugsy. (*SHE leads the seal Off while HAROLD watches. Then HE looks around at all the fascinating things. MAUDE, from Offstage.*) What do you think of my new sculpture?

HAROLD. I like it.

MAUDE. (*popping in for a moment*) No, no, you've got to take your time. Feel it. Touch it. Let the wood talk back to you.

HAROLD. Oh. (*HAROLD tentatively reaches out and moves his hands over the curved and highly polished wood. HE is beginning to enjoy it as MAUDE enters.*)

MAUDE. That's the spirit. What do you think of it now?

HAROLD. It's fun.

MAUDE. Yes. I only finished it last month. It was my trip into the tactile.

HAROLD. Did you do these paintings, too?

MAUDE. Let me see. Yes, that's mine. It's called "Rainbow with Egg Underneath and an Elephant". How's it hit you? (*SHE shows it to him. It is very surreal.*)

HAROLD. Very interesting.

MAUDE. (*doubtfully*) Yes . . . But the nude was by a friend of mine. I modelled for him so he gave it to me as a gift.

HAROLD. (*a little shocked*) That's you?

MAUDE. Yes. Why, don't you like it?

HAROLD. Oh, sure.

MAUDE. But you disapprove?

HAROLD. (*quickly*) Oh, no.

MAUDE. Really? Do you think it's wrong?

HAROLD. (*after thinking it over*) No.

MAUDE. Oh, I'm so glad you said that, Harold. Now I know we're going to be great friends. Come here. I want to show you my "odorifics". (*MAUDE leads him over to a brightly-painted box-like machine, full of lights and switches and a strange little pump on the side.*)

HAROLD. What's that?

MAUDE. Oh, it's a little thing I heard about – a reaction to the indifference with which art treats the nose. I don't know why it's so, but it is. Painting for the eyes, music for the ears, and nothing for the nose. So I decided let's give the old *schnauze* a treat. Have a kind of olfactory banquet. (*SHE looks through some metal cylinders.*) I began on the easiest – roast beef, old books, mown grass – then I went on to these, "An Evening at Maxims", "Mexican Farmyard" . . . Here's one you'd like . . . (*SHE picks it up.*) "Christmas in New York". (*SHE places the cylinder in the box-like machine, pumps it up a little and holds out the hose with the face mask on the end. HAROLD takes it and holds it up to his nose.*) Ready?

(*HE nods. SHE flicks the switch.*)

Okay, what do you smell?

(*HAROLD breathes in slowly and then smiles with
    surprise.*)

HAROLD. Subways!
MAUDE. Go on.
HAROLD. (*breathing again*) Perfume . . . cigarettes . . .
roasting chestnuts . . . *Snow!*

(*MAUDE laughs and turns it off.*)

MAUDE. Oh, yes. You can put together any number of
them. They can be lots of fun.
HAROLD. They're great. Really great. I wonder if I
could make one myself.
MAUDE. Of course you could. And improve on it. I
myself thought of continuing – graduating to the abstract
and free smelling.
HAROLD. (*looking it over*) I'm pretty good with
machines . . . and once I get the basic design . . .
MAUDE. Oh, you'll have no trouble. Sit down. I'll put
on the kettle and we'll have some lunch.
HAROLD. Oh, thank you, but I really can't stay. I have
an appointment.
MAUDE. At the dentist?
HAROLD. Kind of. My mother has arranged it.
MAUDE. Well then, you'll just have to come back and
visit.
HAROLD. All right.
MAUDE. My door is always open.

HAROLD. All right.
MAUDE. Promise?
HAROLD. (*smiling*) I promise. (*HE exits.*)

BLACKOUT

ACT I

Scene 7

PLACE: *HAROLD'S HOUSE.*

MRS. CHASEN is waiting in the living room arranging a vase of daffodils. The MAID enters with HAROLD's first computer date, a cute, blonde, pugnosed student called SYLVIE GAZEL. MRS. CHASEN turns to greet her and the MAID exits.

MRS. CHASEN. Hello, you must be Sylvie Gazel.
SYLVIE. That's right.
MRS. CHASEN. I'm Mrs. Chasen, Harold's mother.
SYLVIE. Nice to meet you.
MRS. CHASEN. I'm so happy you could come over and meet Harold. I was just looking for him. He was in the garden this morning . . .

(THEY go to the French window and look out in the garden.)

SYLVIE. Oh, what lovely daffodils.
MRS. CHASEN. Yes, they're marvellous, aren't they? My

pride and joy . . . Oh, there he is . . . Harold!

HAROLD. (*Offstage*) Yes!

MRS. CHASEN. Come inside. Your first young lady is here from the computer dating club.

HAROLD. (*Offstage*) Oh? Hello.

SYLVIE. Hello. (*SHE waves to him Offstage.*)

MRS. CHASEN. We'll wait for you in the living room.

(*THEY go to the chairs.*)

SYLVIE. He seems very nice.

MRS. CHASEN. I think so. Please, sit down.

SYLVIE. Thank you.

(*MRS. CHASEN sits with her back to the French windows. SYLVIE sits in front of her.*)

MRS. CHASEN. I understand you're at the university?

SYLVIE. Yes. That's right.

MRS. CHASEN. What are you studying?

SYLVIE. "Polly Sigh". With a minor in Home Ec.

MRS. CHASEN. "Polly Sigh"?

SYLVIE. Political Science. It's all about what's going on. Is Harold interested in what's going on? I mean, I think it's such a super thing to study. And then, of course, I can always fall back on my Home Ec—that's Home Economics. You know—how to be a housewife.

MRS. CHASEN. (*vaguely*) Yes. That's good planning.

SYLVIE. Well, it's my life. (*Looking out the French window behind MRS. CHASEN, SYLVIE suddenly sees HAROLD push a large coffin-like chest into view. HE looks at her for a moment, smiles, and exits. SYLVIE is a little nonplussed, but SHE is brought down to earth by MRS.*)

CHASEN.)

Mrs. Chasen. Tell me, Sylvie, are you a regular in this computer club?

Sylvie. Heavens no! I don't have to worry about dates. You see, the other girls in my sorority, well, we decided that somebody should try it so we drew straws and I lost. (*SHE giggles, then adds quickly.*) But I am looking forward to meeting Harold.

(*HAROLD appears in the French window, opens the chest and begins sprinkling the inside with gasoline. SYLVIE watches, fascinated.*)

Mrs. Chasen. Yes. Well, I can't imagine what's keeping him. Would you like some tea, Sylvie?

Sylvie. Eh, what?

Mrs. Chasen. Tea?

Sylvie. Oh, yes. Thank you.

(*MRS. CHASEN pushes the buzzer and the MAID enters.*)

Bring in some tea for us please, Marie. And some of those macaroon cookies I brought home yesterday.

Marie. Yes, Madam. (*SHE looks out the window at HAROLD and the chest.*) Will Master Harold be joining you?

Mrs. Chasen. Yes, in a few minutes.

Marie. (*SHE gives SYLVIE a pitying look.*) Very good, Madam.

(*SHE exits. HAROLD after checking his cigarette lighter steps into the box and lies down closing the lid on top of him. SYLVIE is very puzzled.*)

SYLVIE. Does Harold have any particular . . . hobbies?

MRS. CHASEN. Well, now that you mention it, Sylvie, he does have his little eccentric moments.

SYLVIE. You mean like practical jokes?

MRS. CHASEN. Yes. In a fashion.

(*SYLVIE finally comprehends: chuckling with relief SHE once again becomes her sparkling, bouncing self.*)

SYLVIE. Oh, I understand. I have a little brother who's a terrible prankster too!

MRS. CHASEN. Really?

SYLVIE. Yes. One Sunday he and my Uncle Fred took the old T.V. set from the garage, removed all the parts from it, and set it up in the living room with Uncle Fred crouching behind it. Then he brought in the whole family and – Surprise! – there was Uncle Fred on television reading the six o'clock news. (*SHE laughs*)

MRS. CHASEN. I'm sure that must have been very amusing.

(*SYLVIE looks up in time to see the chest burst into flames. SHE jumps up wildly pointing and screaming.*)

SYLVIE. Har . . . Har . . . Harold!!

(*MRS. CHASEN, not having seen what's happened, thinks SYLVIE has suddenly gone berserk. The MAID enters with the tea tray and sets it down.*)

Harold! Harold! Look. Look!

(*MRS. CHASEN, still confused, glances at the MAID who points to the French window. MRS. CHASEN turns and sees the smoking chest.*)

MRS. CHASEN. Oh, no. (*SHE goes to the window and looks out.*) No! Harold. Harold!

(*HAROLD comes to the doorway buttoning up his jacket.*)

HAROLD. Yes.

MRS. CHASEN. (*turning angrily*) You left your corpse in the daffodils.

(*SYLVIE emits a horrible cry and begins to sob convulsively. MRS. CHASEN, the MAID and HAROLD stop to look at her for a moment before SHE bursts into tears and runs from the room. There is a moment of quiet, as the THREE exchange glances. Then the MAID takes one cup from the tea tray and exits.*)

BLACKOUT

ACT I

Scene 8

PLACE: *MAUDE'S HOUSE.*

INSPECTOR BERNARD, a tall, tough cop and his fat little assistant, SERGEANT DOPPEL, enter with a rather reluctant FATHER FINNEGAN. BERNARD had apparently just seen the little PRIEST's car Off-stage. THEY stand outside MAUDE's house.

BERNARD. That is your car, then?

PRIEST. Oh, yes. That's my car all right.

BERNARD. Mark that down, Doppel, positive identification. We'll get you to sign it, and we can take out a warrant then on Madame Chardin.

PRIEST. You mean, arrest her?

BERNARD. That's right. We've had dealings with her before but every time we think we've got her she manages somehow to talk her way out of it. But don't worry, Padre. She won't be able to talk her way out of this.

(HAROLD enters.)

Hey, who are you?

HAROLD. What? Oh, hello, Father.

BERNARD. I said who are you?

PRIEST. That's Harold Chasen, the boy I was telling you about.

BERNARD. The one who drove off with the old lady? Take his name down, Doppel.

HAROLD. What is all this? Where's Maude?

BERNARD. That's what we were just going to ask you.

HAROLD. I don't know.

BERNARD. Are you a friend of hers?

HAROLD. *(hesitatingly)* Well, I . . .

BERNARD. Come on, kid, it's a simple "yes" or "no". Are you a friend of hers?

HAROLD. *(making a decision)* Yes.

BERNARD. Mark that down, Doppel—and you better run a check on him for any outstanding violations.

(*DOPPEL exits*)

HAROLD. I haven't done anything.

BERNARD. Maybe not. But your friend has just been accused of stealing a car.

PRIEST. Eh, I've been thinking it over, Inspector, and I don't want to make a big fuss. I've got the car back now and don't you think it would be better if we could just drop the whole thing?

BERNARD. What! Listen, Padre, I've been waiting to pin something on this gal for a long time. You just can't walk out on me.

PRIEST. But the publicity and the trial – Surely if she promises never to do it again?

BERNARD. You don't seem to realize, a crime has been committed. That's not something to be taken lightly.

PRIEST. Oh, no. I'll speak to her – very firmly. But I don't think we want to prosecute.

BERNARD. (*reluctantly*) Okay, Father. If that's your decision. But just remember that it's you who'll have to take responsibility for the next far-out crazy stunt she pulls.

(*DOPPEL enters hurriedly.*)

What is it, Doppel?

DOPPEL. It just came over the radio, Sir. We're wanted at the zoo right away.

BERNARD. The zoo?

DOPPEL. Yes, Sir. They've just reported a stolen seal.

HAROLD. What? (*HE looks nervously around for the seal.*)

BERNARD. My God, a seal. There are more nuts in this

town than I thought. Okay, let's go. (*to HAROLD*) But you tell your friend from me that one day she is going to slip up and when she does I'm going to throw the book at her. (*HE and DOPPEL exit.*)

PRIEST. I think he means what he says, Harold, so you'd better tell her to be careful.

HAROLD. (*wanting him to go*) Yes, Father.

PRIEST. I know she means well but her impulsiveness is going to land her in trouble.

HAROLD. Okay, Father, I'll tell her.

PRIEST. After all she just can't keep taking things. There are rules.

(*MAUDE enters carrying a bouquet of daisies.*)

MAUDE. Hello, Harold—how nice to see you again—and Father Finnegan! What a wonderful surprise. Had any interesting burials lately?

PRIEST. Madam, I'm afraid this isn't a social call. I have something important to tell you.

MAUDE. How exciting. Let's go inside.

HAROLD. (*quickly*) No!

(*MAUDE and FATHER FINNEGAN stop and stare at him.*)

I mean it's very nice out here . . . very peaceful . . . (*meaningfully to MAUDE*) No animals.

MAUDE. (*laughing*) Harold, what are you talking about? Come inside, Father, we can have a nice hot cup of tea. (*SHE goes inside the house and the PRIEST follows. HAROLD shrugs and goes in too.*)

PRIEST. All I want to say is that you are a very lucky

woman.

MAUDE. I know that, Father.

PRIEST. I have decided not to prosecute.

MAUDE. Prosecute what?

PRIEST. You took my car off yesterday. Don't you remember?

MAUDE. What did it look like?

PRIEST. Blue Volkswagen—white wall tires—a St. Christopher medal on the dashboard.

MAUDE. Oh, yes. I remember now. The brakes were a little soft. Have you ever had oat straw tea, Father, I recommend it highly.

PRIEST. Please, madam, this is not a subject to be taken lightly. A car is a serious affair.

MAUDE. You think so? I could never really get enthused over them. They're to be driven, that's all. It's not as if it were alive—like a horse, or a camel. By the way where's Mister Murgatroyd? Have you seen him?

PRIEST. Mister Murgatroyd?

HAROLD. He's . . . He's in the bathroom, but I'm sure he doesn't want to be disturbed.

MAUDE. Nonsense, he loves people to watch him in the bath. Come on, let's go watch.

PRIEST. Madam!

MAUDE. Where's his ball? (*SHE starts looking*)

HAROLD. (*trying to stop the inevitable*) Maude, I really don't think we should go in there . . .

MAUDE. Harold, what's the matter with you? You saw how friendly he is. (*SHE finds a huge colored beach ball.*) Here, Father, take this ball and if you ask him nicely he'll sit up in the bath and balance it on his nose.

PRIEST. Madam!

MAUDE. Mugsy! Mugsy! (*SHE opens the bathroom door*

and goes inside. Offstage) You've finished have you, darling? Well, come on outside and say hello to my friends. *(MAUDE enters leading the seal. HAROLD glances at the PRIEST who opens his mouth with horror.)*

PRIEST. Oh, sweet mother of God!

MAUDE. I beg your pardon, Father?

PRIEST. That's a seal!

MAUDE. That's right, Mister Murgatroyd, say hello to Father Finnegan.

(The seal barks, MAUDE laughs.)

He likes you, Father. Go ahead and throw him the ball. Go on, he loves to play. No one ever plays with him at the zoo.

PRIEST. I knew it! I knew it! Oh, sweet mother of God! *(HE collapses in a chair.)*

MAUDE. What's the matter? Aren't you feeling well?

PRIEST. It's nothing. Nothing. Just a little lightness in the head.

MAUDE. Harold, go get him a glass of water.

PRIEST. No, it's all right. I've got to be going. But you . . . you took that seal from the zoo?

MAUDE. Yes. If you would have seen the water in that cage – filthy, polluted and hardly any room at all – I just knew I had to take him to the ocean and set him free.

HAROLD. But, Maude, the police were by here just now. They know all about it.

MAUDE. You mean Inspector Bernard and that cute little Sergeant Doppel? I'm sorry I missed them.

HAROLD. But aren't you afraid . . .

MAUDE. Of them? *(SHE laughs.)* When it comes to police I've been through them all. But I suppose we must think of Mugsy. (*to the seal*) I'm sorry, sweetie, but we'll have to cut your visit short. I've got to take you to the beach this afternoon. What's that? (*SHE laughs.*) Harold take him in the kitchen. He's always hungry after a bath.

(*HAROLD exits with the seal.*)

Oh, and bring the champagne from the fridge.

PRIEST. Let me get this straight for a moment . . . You're going to take that stolen seal to the beach and release him into the ocean?

MAUDE. Yes. That's right. Would you like to come with us?

PRIEST. (*getting up quickly*) No. No. Thank you. I've got other engagements. I'll be busy all afternoon.

MAUDE. Oh, how fortunate! Then you wouldn't mind if we take your car. (*MAUDE exits and the PRIEST collapses back in the chair.*)

BLACKOUT

ACT I

Scene 9

PLACE: *THE BEACH.*

HAROLD and MAUDE are facing the ocean and, to the sound of surf and seagulls, THEY are waving farewell to the seal. MAUDE's basket, her daisies and a bottle of champagne are nearby.

MAUDE. Goodbye, Mister Murgatroyd.

HAROLD. Goodbye.

MAUDE. He looks so happy. And he swims so well, don't you think, Harold? – all that rolling over and flopping about. (*SHE looks out again.*) *Mugsy!* (*SHE lets out with her piercing whistle and shouts:*) You're going the wrong way. *Swim north!* (*SHE smiles.*) Ah, that's better. We want him to find his friends.

HAROLD. Maude, how do you do that whistle?

MAUDE. It's very easy, Harold. See, you take these two fingers, put the ends together and place them just beneath the tip of the tongue. Then push the tongue backward till your lips close on the first knuckle. Now tighten your lips and blow.

(*HAROLD, who has been following these instructions, blows. A faint whistle comes out.*)

That's right. But keep your tongue curled.

(*HAROLD blows again. This time it is a little better.*)

You're getting it. Just keep that up and practice. My elder brother taught me how to do that when I was just a little girl. He never thought I could learn it but after a while I could do it better than he.

HAROLD. It's a new trick for me.

MAUDE. Good. Try something new each day, that's my motto. After all, we're given life to find it out. It doesn't last forever.

HAROLD. You look as if you could.

MAUDE. Me? Ha! Did I tell you I'll be eighty on Saturday?

HAROLD. You don't look eighty.

MAUDE. That's the influence of the right food, the right exercise, and the right breathing. Greet the dawn with "The Breath of Fire." Like this. (*SHE demonstrates and the exercise leaves her a little winded. SHE laughs.*) Of course, there's no doubt the body is giving out. I'm well into autumn. I'll have to be giving it all up after Saturday. (*thoughtfully*) Do you sing?

HAROLD. What's that?

MAUDE. Do you sing and dance?

HAROLD. Eh, no.

MAUDE. No. I thought not. (*SHE smiles.*) Tell me about yourself, Harold. What do you do when you aren't visiting funerals?

HAROLD. Oh, a lot of things. I work on my projects in my room.

MAUDE. And what else?

HAROLD. On Thursday, for example, I go to the junk yard. That's the day they crush up all the old cars into compressed little cubes of metal. It's fascinating. I'll take you to see it if you like?

MAUDE. I'd love to. We'll go tomorrow and in return I'll take you to a flower farm. Ever been to a flower farm, Harold?

HAROLD. Never.

MAUDE. That's a treat. Flowers are so friendly.

HAROLD. Really?

MAUDE. Yes. I was there this morning. Flowers are so empathetic. (*SHE picks up the bouquet of daisies.*) They grow and bloom and fade and die and change into something else. Isn't that thrilling?

HAROLD. Yes. It's all change, I imagine.

MAUDE. Absolutely! And I think if I had my choice

I would like to change into a sunflower most of all.

HAROLD. Why's that?

MAUDE. Because they're bright, and simple and . . . (*slyly*) because they're tall. (*SHE laughs.*) When I was a girl that was my greatest wish – to grow long. It never happened and I could do nothing about it, except make up my mind it wasn't going to stop me. It hasn't. Still, I can't help thinking it might have been fun. (*SHE laughs.*) What about you, Harold? What flower would you like to be?

HAROLD. I don't know. I'm just an ordinary person. Maybe one of those. (*HE points to the bouquet SHE is holding.*)

MAUDE. Why do you say that?

HAROLD. I guess because they're all the same.

MAUDE. Oh, but they're not. Look here. See. Some are smaller, some are fatter, some grow to the left, some to the right, some even have some petals missing – all kinds of observable differences, and we haven't even touched the biochemical. You know, to me they're just like the Japanese. At first you think they all look alike, but after you get to know them, you see there is not a repeat in the bunch. Each person is different, never existed before and never to exist again. Just like this flower . . . (*SHE picks one out and shows it to him.*) An individual!

HAROLD. Well, we may be individuals, all right, but we have to grow up together.

MAUDE. That's very true. Still, I believe that much of this world's sorrow comes from people who know they are *this* . . . (*showing him the flower*) . . . yet let themselves be treated as *that*. (*SHE sadly holds up the bouquet of flowers in her other hand and turns with tears in her*

*eyes to HAROLD. THEY look at each other for a moment
and then SHE smiles.*) Well, let's go off to the hospital
and see my friend, Pablo. He needs cheering up.

(*HAROLD picks up her old basket and a bottle of
    champagne.*)

Do you like champagne?
   HAROLD. Well, I really don't drink.
   MAUDE. Oh, it's all right. It's organic.
   HAROLD. Okay. (*HE smiles.*) It will be my new ex-
perience for today.
   MAUDE. That's wonderful, Harold. And tomorrow we'll
learn how to yodel.

(*THEY exit to the sounds of yodelling.*)

BLACKOUT

ACT I

Scene 10

PLACE: *HAROLD'S HOUSE.*

*MRS. CHASEN and HAROLD's second computer date
    are sitting in the living room having tea. This is
    NANCY MERSCH, a bespectacled little girl with close-
    ly cropped brown hair and an overly anxious willing-
    ness to please.*

Mrs. Chasen. Milk?
Nancy. No, thank you.
Mrs. Chasen. Sugar?
Nancy. No, thank you . . . well, all right.
Mrs. Chasen. One lump?
Nancy. Two. Thank you.

(*MRS. CHASEN hands her the cup.*)

Thank you.
　Mrs. Chasen. Well now, Nancy, I understand you're
a secretary.
　Nancy. That's right. Harrison Feed and Grain.
　Mrs. Chasen. And what exactly does that entail?
　Nancy. Well, I get to work at eight-thirty – sometimes
eight-forty if I don't catch my bus – but that's all right,
because Mr. Harrison never gets in before nine. In fact,
Sheila says – that's Sheila Farenheit, my friend who works
across the hall at Henderson Tool and Dye – eh, that's
nothing to do with us, of course, although sometimes our
mail gets sent there and their mail gets sent to us . . .
I mean, Harrison Feed and Grain – Henderson Tool and
Dye – they are sort of the same but, of course, we're in
absolutely different businesses altogether. Sheila and I
sometimes have a laugh over that.
　Mrs. Chasen. Well, it sounds very interesting.
　Nancy. Oh, yes. It can be very challenging.
　Mrs. Chasen. I don't know what on earth is keeping
Harold. (*SHE buzzes.*) He knows you are here and he
was just going upstairs to change his shirt.

(*The MAID enters.*)

Marie, go upstairs and tell Harold to hurry. Nancy is waiting to meet him.

NANCY. (*sweetly*) Yes.

(*The MAID gives NANCY a pitying look and exits.*)

MRS. CHASEN. Have you always lived in this area, Nancy?

NANCY. Yes. I was born here, went to school here, and now I'm working here. (*SHE giggles.*) I'm just a homebody, I guess. But as my daddy says, "Don't be too eager to leave home. That will come soon enough." (*SHE laughs pleasantly. MRS. CHASEN, politely, joins in. THEY sip their tea when suddenly a loud rifle shot from upstairs rents the air. NANCY is startled and looks over at MRS. CHASEN. After glancing up with momentary displeasure, MRS. CHASEN smiles reassuringly at NANCY. Picking up the teapot, SHE decides to ignore the entire incident.*)

MRS. CHASEN. More tea, Nancy?

NANCY. Well, no . . . Oh, all right. Thank you.

MRS. CHASEN. Your father sounds very nice. What does he do for a living?

NANCY. He's retired now. He used to work for television.

MRS. CHASEN. (*impressed*) Really?

NANCY. Yes. He used to put the antennas on the roof. But after my sister Gloria got married last April—no, it was the April before—remember when we had all that rain? It rained the day of the wedding, too, but as my daddy said to me—I was one of the bridesmaids—"After the rain comes the sunshine", and I suppose it does because now she lives in Saudi Arabia. Her husband is in oil.

(*MRS. CHASEN gives an odd smile and looks over at the clock.*)

I can't imagine what's keeping Harold. He said he was going to put on a clean shirt and . . .

(*The door opens and the MAID enters carrying a blood-stained shirt. MRS. CHASEN and NANCY stare at her and wait for an explanation. SHE opens her mouth when suddenly an even louder gun shot echoes Offstage.*)

HAROLD. (*Offstage*) Damnit!

(*NANCY reacts nervously and looks over at MRS. CHASEN. The MAID turns back to them both.*)

MARIE. Master Harold will be down in a minute, Madam. He said he's having a little trouble dressing. (*SHE drapes the blood-stained shirt over her arm and exits. NANCY is very bewildered and anxious but MRS. CHASEN takes a deep breath and continues as if nothing out of the ordinary has happened.*)
MRS. CHASEN. More tea, Nancy?
NANCY. Well . . . I don't . . . What was . . . Oh, all right. Thank you.

(*MRS. CHASEN pours.*)

MRS. CHASEN. Two sugars?
NANCY. Three.
MRS. CHASEN. Tell me, Nancy, how did you find out about the computer club?

NANCY. The club? Oh, that's a very funny story. Last month, my girlfriend Sheila—I told you about her—she works across the hall—well she was going out with this boy Arthur, he plays the clarinet. Well, Arthur has a twin brother called Arnold who just happens to be one of the drivers who works for us. You know we have a trucking fleet of ten, sometimes twelve, trucks. In fact, I type up the schedules every week, usually on Monday mornings unless I still have the invoices to do from the previous Friday . . . in which case I . . .

(*A loud gunshot immediately Offstage makes NANCY jump and turn around. The door opens and HAROLD enters with a smoking rifle. Disgusted, HE puts it down on a table, and walking over to his mother and NANCY, HE stands before them as if HE had merely laid down his tennis racket after a bad game. MRS. CHASEN is the first to regain her composure. SHE gestures to the shaken NANCY.*)

MRS. CHASEN. Harold, dear, I'd like you to meet Nancy Mersch. Nancy this is my son, Harold.
NANCY. Hello. I'm very pleased to make your acquaintance.
HAROLD. Hello.
MRS. CHASEN. Sit down, Harold, and I'll pour you some tea. Nancy was just telling me about . . . what was it about, dear?

(*HAROLD sits with his left hand on a small end table. NANCY is trying to ignore the rifle.*)

NANCY. The invoices. (*to HAROLD*) I type up the invoices on Mondays.

MRS. CHASEN. Yes. Nancy is a secretary at Henderson Feed and Grain.

NANCY. No, *Harrison, Harrison* Feed and Grain.

MRS. CHASEN. Oh.

NANCY. You were probably thinking of *Henderson* Tool and Dye. (*to HAROLD*) It's a common mistake. They're across the hall with my friend Sheila Farenheit.

(*HAROLD nods pleasantly, takes out a cleaver and cuts off his hand at the wrist. MRS. CHASEN stops pouring tea and glances at the cleaver embedded in the table while NANCY's eyes bulge at the sight of the severed hand with total incomprehension. HAROLD looks blandly over at his mother who takes a deep breath and decides to make the best of a bad situation. SHE smiles sweetly at the white-faced GIRL.*)

MRS. CHASEN. More tea, Nancy?

(*NANCY blinks like a patient coming out of sedation. SHE smiles weakly at MRS. CHASEN and carefully puts her cup down on the table.*)

NANCY. I . . . I think I'm not feeling . . . Excuse . . . (*SHE stands up unsteadily and with another vague smile starts politely for the door. SHE manages one step before collapsing under the table like a limp rag doll.*)

BLACKOUT

ACT I

Scene 11

PLACE: *THE PSYCHIATRIST'S AREA*

DOCTOR. (*on the phone*) What?! . . . Is that a fact, Helen?
The first girl . . . hmmm . . . and the second girl . . .
a cleaver! What was that he cut off? . . .

(*The LIGHTS COME UP on MRS. CHASEN'S area.
SHE is talking to the DOCTOR on the phone.*)

MRS. CHASEN. His left hand.
DOCTOR. Oh, thank God.
MRS. CHASEN. Not to mention the damage he did to
the table! I must say, doctor, I had hoped to see a little
more sign of improvement.
DOCTOR. So had I, but . . .
MRS. CHASEN. When are you seeing him again?
DOCTOR. But don't you know? Harold cancelled all his
appointments this morning.
MRS. CHASEN. All of them?
DOCTOR. That's right. He said he didn't think he'd be
needing a psychiatrist anymore.
MRS. CHASEN. Oh, Lord. Where am I to turn? My

brother, the general, says that only the Army can make a man out of him.

DOCTOR. Really? Well, judging from what I know about Harold I'd say he has all the qualities for a successful military career.

BLACKOUT

ACT I

Scene 12

PLACE: *MAUDE'S HOUSE.*

It is raining outside in the night but inside all is warm and cozy. HAROLD and MAUDE have just finished a Japanese type dinner sitting on cushions around a table on the floor. THEY are both in kimonos and MAUDE stands up to show hers off. (It is inspired by the painting by Monet.)

MAUDE. It was made for me in Yokhohama—with matching fan.

HAROLD. It's beautiful. I'm glad we decided to eat Oriental. It was a perfect dinner.

MAUDE. Well, it was a perfect day. Walking around the flower farm in the rain—I couldn't imagine anything more delightful.

HAROLD. (*laughing*) We were soaked. We should have taken that umbrella up there.

(*MAUDE turns to look at the old umbrella hanging over the fireplace.*)

MAUDE. Oh, yes. Look at that. Goodness, I haven't noticed that in years. (*SHE takes it down.*) It used to be my defense on picket lines, and rallies, and political meetings—being dragged off by the police or attacked by the thugs of the opposition. Oh my. (*SHE laughs.*) That was a long time ago.

HAROLD. What were you fighting for?

MAUDE. Oh, big issues. Liberty. Rights. Justice? Kings died and kingdoms fell. You know, I don't regret the kingdoms—I see no sense in borders and nations and patriotism—but I do miss the kings. When I was a little girl in Vienna, I was taken to the palace for a garden party. I can still see the sunshine on the fountains, the parasols, and the flashing uniforms of the young officers. I thought then I would marry a soldier. (*SHE chuckles.*) Oh, my. How Frederick would chide me about that. He was so serious, so very tall and proper. Being a doctor at the university, and in the government, he thought dignity was in how you wore your hat. That's how we met. I knocked off his hat. With a snowball in the Volksgarten. (*SHE smiles softly and gazes into the fire.*) But that was all . . . before.

(*HAROLD looks at her not knowing what to say. SHE seems suddenly very small and fragile.*)

HAROLD. (*after a moment*) So you don't use the umbrella anymore?

MAUDE. (*looking up at him*) No. Not anymore.

HAROLD. No more revolts?

MAUDE. Oh yes! Every day. But I don't need a defense anymore. I embrace! Still fighting for the Big Issues, but now in my small, individual way. (*SHE smiles warmly and takes a hookah standing beside her.*) How about a smoke?
HAROLD. Well, I really don't think I . . .
MAUDE. It's all right. It's organic.
HAROLD. Okay.

(*MAUDE lights the large brass hookah and hands one
       of the hoses to HAROLD.*)

MAUDE. Here you are. Take a toke.

(*HAROLD takes the hose and inhales. HE smiles.*)

HAROLD. I'm sure picking up on vices.
MAUDE. Vice? Virtue? It's best not to be too moral. You cheat yourself out of too much life. Aim above morality. As Confucius says, "Don't simply be good. Make good things happen."
HAROLD. Did Confucius say that?
MAUDE. Well. (*SHE smiles.*) They say he was very wise, so I'm sure he must have.

(*HAROLD takes another drag on the pipe. HE looks
       at MAUDE intently.*)

HAROLD. You are the wisest person I know.
MAUDE. Me! Ha! When I look around me, I know I know nothing. I remember, though, once long ago in Persia we met a wise man in the bazaar. He was a professional and his specialty for tourists was a maxim engraved

on the head of a pin—"The wisest", he said, "the truest, the most instructive words for all men at all times." Frederick bought one for me and back at the hotel I peered through a magnifying glass to read what it said: "And this too shall pass away." (*SHE laughs.*) And the wise man was right. Apply that, and you're bound to live life fully.

(*HAROLD takes a thoughtful drag.*)

HAROLD. Yes, I haven't lived. (*HE suddenly giggles.*) I've died a few times.
MAUDE. What was that?
HAROLD. Died. Seventeen times—not counting maimings. (*HE laughs wildly.*) Shot myself in the head once with a popgun and a pellet of blood.
MAUDE. How ingenious! Tell me about them.
HAROLD. Well, it's a question of timing and the right equipment . . . You really want to hear about this?
MAUDE. Of course.
HAROLD. (*grinning*) Okay. The first time it wasn't even planned. I was at boarding school trying out some experiments in the chemistry lab. I was mixing this stuff together—all very scientific—when suddenly there was this massive explosion! Pow! It blew a hole in the floor, knocked me down, singed my hair. I got up—smoke and flames everywhere. I just wanted to get out of there. Fortunately there was an old laundry chute in the wall so I slid down it to the basement. When I got outside— Wow!—The whole top of the building was on fire. Alarms were ringing and people shouting so I decided I'd better go home. (*HE sits down by MAUDE.*) When I got there my mother was giving a party, so I crept up the back

stairs to my room. Then there was a ring at the front door. It was the police. I leaned over the banister and heard them tell my mother that I had died in an accident at school. I couldn't see her face, but she looked at the people around her and began to stagger . . . She put one hand to her forehead. With the other she reached out, as if groping for support. Two men rushed to her side, and then – with a long, long sigh – she collapsed in their arms. (*HE stops for a long pause.*) . . . I decided then I enjoyed being dead.

(*MAUDE says nothing for a moment. Then SHE speaks softly.*)

MAUDE. Yes, I understand. A lot of people enjoy being dead. But they're not dead, really. They're just backing away from life. (*SHE jumps up and shouts out like a cheerleader.*) Reach out! Take a chance! Get hurt, maybe – but play as well as you can. Go, team, go! Give me an "L". Give me an "I". Give me a "V". Give me an "E". L-I-V-E. LIVE! (*SHE sits down quietly.*) Otherwise, you'll have nothing to talk about in the locker room.

(*HAROLD smiles at her.*)

HAROLD. I like you, Maude.

(*MAUDE smiles back.*)

MAUDE. I like you, too, Harold. Let's have a song.
HAROLD. A song?
MAUDE. (*going over to the piano*) Now don't tell me you can't sing. Everybody can sing – even me. (*MAUDE

sits down at the piano and begins to play a song. [See author's Notes on Staging.] She sings it through once and asks HAROLD to join in for the second chorus. HE does so and THEY finish with a joyous two part harmony. HAROLD laughs and claps his hands.) Oh, that was fun. Let's play something together.

HAROLD. But I don't play anything.

MAUDE. Not anything! Dear me, who was in charge of your education? Everyone should be able to make some music. It's the universal language, the cosmic dance. Let me see what I can find. *(SHE goes to a large cupboard which is full of all kinds of musical instruments. After rooting about for a while, SHE pulls out a banjo and gives it to him.)* This will be perfect. *(SHE shows him how to play it.)* You hold it like this and put your fingers there like that. Good.

(HAROLD strums a couple of chords.)

HAROLD. It doesn't sound much like music.

MAUDE. Oh, you've got to make friends with it first. Put in some time and get to know each other. Then when you become one let the music flow out of you as freely as though you were dancing. *(SHE sits down at the piano and begins playing "The Merry Widow Waltz." After the first chorus SHE bangs the Chinese gong on top of the piano and the piano begins to play by itself. MAUDE stands up and waltzes about the room while HAROLD looks around delightedly wondering where the music is coming from.)*

HAROLD. How do you do that?

MAUDE. Oh, it's very easy. *(SHE demonstrates the*

dance.) One-two-three. One-two-three. (*A full orchestra joins in the second chorus, and MAUDE holds out her hands to HAROLD.*) Shall we waltz?

(*HAROLD smiles and takes her in his arms. Together THEY waltz around the room as the curtain falls.*)

END OF ACT I

ACT II

Scene 1

Place: *HAROLD'S HOUSE.*

*The curtain opens to reveal HAROLD sitting in the living
   room practicing the song Maude taught him on his
   banjo. After a few moments, MRS. CHASEN enters.*

Mrs. Chasen. I've just seen your last computer date
drive up—Harold, put that thing away and listen to me.
She'll be here in a minute and I want you to assure me
again that we will have no repetition of the previous ex-
periences. I'm going to leave you alone with her and I
don't want to have to come back in the room to find her
hysterically holding up your head or your hand. Is that
clear?

Harold. Yes, mother.

Mrs. Chasen. After all, if you think you can do without
Doctor Mathews, this is your chance to show it.

Harold. Yes, mother.

Mrs. Chasen. Be polite. Be a gentleman. And kindly
remember that this girl is your third and final chance.

(The MAID shows in SUNSHINE DORE and exits.

*SUNSHINE is a lanky, red-haired girl in boots
with a sassy manner and a "been around" look.)*

Hello. You must be . . . eh . . .

SUNSHINE. Sunshine Dore.

HAROLD. How do you do?

SUNSHINE. Can't complain.

MRS. CHASEN. I remember. You're the actress, aren't
you?

SUNSHINE. I like to think so.

MRS. CHASEN. Well, I'm sure you and Harold will have
a lot to talk about. He's very interested in theatrics.

SUNSHINE. Groovy.

MRS. CHASEN. I'll go and get some drinks. Harold,
perhaps Starlight would like a cigarette.

SUNSHINE. That's *Sunshine*.

MRS. CHASEN. Yes, of course. (*MRS. CHASEN exits.
HAROLD leads SUNSHINE over to the couch and THEY
sit. There is a momentary pause.)*

HAROLD. Would you like a cigarette?

SUNSHINE. No, thank you. They stain my fingers.

HAROLD. Oh. (*A pause. HAROLD is really trying to
make conversation.)* Is Sunshine your real name?

SUNSHINE. Actually, it was the name of my drama
teacher – Louis Sunshine. Perhaps you've heard of him?

HAROLD. No.

SUNSHINE. Well, he was such an influence on the
development of my instrument – that means my body in
theatre talk – that when I felt the need to express the
emerging me in a new form, I took on "Sunshine". As
a tribute. Doré is my real name. Well, Dore, actually.
(*SHE gets up.*) Gee, what a lovely place you have here.
I mean it's beautifully furnished. Reminds me of the set

we used for *Macbeth*. (*quickly*) Oh, we did it in modern dress. (*SHE sees the banjo.*) Do you play.

HAROLD. I'm learning. Do you?

SUNSHINE. Not really. I studied guitar for a while, but I had to give it up. Gave me callouses on my fingers. As an actress, I can't afford to have a tarnished instrument.

HAROLD. No, I suppose not. (*A pause. HAROLD tries again.*) Do you do a lot of acting?

SUNSHINE. Oh sure, I practice every day. That's the Sunshine Method – keeping your instrument finely tuned. Lately, I've been working mostly on the classics. Shakespeare, Shaw – I've been studying Cleopatra. I want to do it with an Egyptian accent.

(*HAROLD sighs. SUNSHINE walks over to the mantel-piece.*)

Gee, what a lovely collection of knives. We had a display like this when we did Ibsen's *The Seagull*. May I see them?

HAROLD. (*takes a deep breath*) That's it. (*HE stands up and goes over to her.*)

SUNSHINE. That's what?

HAROLD. That's a really good collection of knives.

SUNSHINE. Really?

HAROLD. Really. (*HE takes one down.*) This knife for example is very interesting. It's a hara-kiri blade.

SUNSHINE. Ohhh. What's hara-kiri?

HAROLD. An ancient Japanese ceremony.

SUNSHINE. Like a tea ceremony?

HAROLD. No. Like this. (*With an Oriental scream, HAROLD plunges the knife in his belly. HE drops to his knees and, bleeding profusely, continues the gouging before*

*tumbling forward with a death-like shudder. SUNSHINE
stares at the lifeless body, then drops to her knees with a
loud groan.)*

SUNSHINE. Oh, Harold. That was marvelous! It had the
ring of truth. Harold. Please. Who did you study with?
(*SHE draws back suddenly.*) I'm sorry, Harold. I don't
want to break into your private moment. I know how ex-
hausting true emotion can be. I played Juliet at the Sunshine Playhouse. Louis thought it was my best perfor-
mance. (*SUNSHINE quickly rearranges her hair and with
a deep breath plunges herself into the role of Juliet mourn-
ing over the death of Romeo.*) What's here? A cup! Closed
in my true love's hand? Poison, I see, hath been his
timeless end. Oh, churl! (*SHE whacks HAROLD.*) Drunk
all, and left no friendly drop to help me after? I will kiss
thy lips.

(*HAROLD opens his eyes, terrified, but SUNSHINE
      continues.*)

Happily some poison yet doth hang on them to make me
die with a restorative. (*SHE kisses HAROLD who immediately kneels up.*) Thy lips are warm.
HAROLD. Eh . . .
SUNSHINE. Yea, noise! Then I'll be brief. (*picking up
the knife*) Oh, happy dagger! (*SHE stops suddenly to test
the knife, pushing the blade into the handle and seeing how
it squirts blood. Satisfied, SHE continues.*) Oh, happy dagger! This is thy sheath. There rest . . . and . . . let . . .
me . . . DIE! (*SHE stabs herself and collapses like a corpse
on the floor. HAROLD is horror-struck. HE has never seen
anything like it. HE stands over her bloody body, completely bewildered. The MAID enters with a vacuum cleaner.*

SHE walks by HAROLD, looks down at SUNSHINE and exits with barely a change of expression. But suddenly we hear a scream. MRS. CHASEN stands wide-eyed in the doorway and drops her tray of drinks.)

MRS. CHASEN. Harold! (*SHE flings out an arm at the lifeless girl.*) That was your last *date!*

BLACKOUT

ACT II

Scene 2

PLACE: *MAUDE'S HOUSE.*

MAUDE is outside her place watering her ferns when INSPECTOR BERNARD and SERGEANT DOP-PEL enter.

MAUDE. Good day, Inspector. And Sergeant Doppel. How nice of you to drop by. I'm sorry I missed you the other day but . . .

BERNARD. (*interrupting*) Madam, we are here on a serious matter. Please pay attention because I don't think you're going to be able to talk yourself out of this one . . . Have you ever heard of Barkley Brothers' Furniture?

MAUDE. (*thoughtfully*) Eh . . . Should I?

BERNARD. Yes, you should. That's where all your furniture came from.

MAUDE. Oh, yes, I remember. A charming little salesman with a nervous twitch in one eye. We had some long talks together. Do you know he really wanted to sail off to the South Seas and photograph parrots and tortoise shells?

BERNARD. Was this man called Eliot, Quincy Eliot?

MAUDE. Yes, that was his name. I wonder whatever became of him?

BERNARD. From what we can gather he shipped out on a freighter for Samoa.

MAUDE. How marvellous! I always said he should do that. It was the only way to get rid of that twitch.

BERNARD. That may be, but he left his papers in such disorder that Barkley Brothers is only now straightening them out. Which brings me to you. Here is a list of furniture that was delivered to this house. (*HE hands her the list.*) There is, however, no indication of payment of any sort. Now unless you can make that payment at once. I have a court order here to authorize the repossession of the said furniture, without further delay. Do you have the money?

MAUDE. No.

BERNARD. I didn't think you would. (*HE takes back the list and calls out to TWO MOVERS Offstage.*) Okay, guys. Take everything on this list.

(*TWO MOVERS enter, take the list from BERNARD and enter the house. During the remainder of the scene, we see them walk off with MAUDE's couch, her table, and her chairs. MAUDE, of course, is not at all dismayed.*)

MAUDE. Are you going to take everything?
BERNARD. Everything.
MAUDE. Oh.

BERNARD. I'm not going to pretend that this is not giving me a certain amount of pleasure. You know that you've been a thorn in my side for some time. But I'm not an unfeeling man. There is an old folks home run by the county and if you sell this house I'm sure . . .

MAUDE. This house?

BERNARD. Yes.

MAUDE. But isn't it on the list?

BERNARD. What?

MAUDE. This house. I seem to remember it came with the furniture.

BERNARD. This isn't your house?

MAUDE. Oh, no.

BERNARD. But that's . . . that's . . . Doppel! I'm leaving you in charge. I'm going back to the station and check on her story.

MAUDE. It's true, inspector.

BERNARD. If it is, then by God tomorrow you'll be looking for a new house (*HE exits.*)

MAUDE. Tomorrow's my birthday. That will all work out just fine. I was planning to move on anyway.

(*HAROLD enters with his banjo. HE is stunned at the sight of the MOVERS carrying off MAUDE's furniture.*)

Hello, Harold, come join the fun. Tell me, sergeant, how long do you think this will take?

DOPPEL. What we don't take by tonight we'll take tomorrow.

MAUDE. Oh, good. That will give me time to get rid of some of these other things.

HAROLD. Maude, what's going on here? Why are they

moving your furniture?

MAUDE. They're clearing out the house. Repossessing, I think they called it. How would you like one of my paintings, sergeant? I think you could use a little color in your life.

HAROLD. But, Maude, how are you going to live in an empty house?

MAUDE. It's all right, Harold. The house is going too. Come on, inside, sergeant. You can have the pick of my collection. Oh, this is exciting. It will be nice to know that all these things are off to live in new homes. Do you think the inspector would like something – this bird feeder, for example?

DOPPEL. I don't think so.

MAUDE. Well, how about this bird bath or maybe a fern . . . Oh, Harold, *look* we still haven't planted the little tree.

HAROLD. Maude . . .

MAUDE. No, no. We've got to do that right away. Pick it up, and I'll go get a shovel. Excuse us, sergeant, this is urgent business. If you want us for anything or if there are any problems – we'll be in the forest. (*SHE exits.*)

DOPPEL. (*nervously*) Do you think it's all right if I take this bird bath for myself?

HAROLD. (*puts down his banjo and wearily picks up the tree*) Sergeant, she wouldn't care if you sat in it naked and balanced a ball on your nose. (*HE exits.*)

BLACKOUT

ACT II

Scene 3

Place: *THE FOREST.*

*The sun is streaming down through the pine trees as
HAROLD and MAUDE finish planting the little tree.
MAUDE pats the earth around its trunk and stands
up.*

Maude. There we are. I think it will be very happy
here.

Harold. It's a nice spot. Good soil.

Maude. Yes, it is. I like the feel of soil, don't you? And
the smell. It's the earth. "The earth is my body. My head
is in the stars." Who said that?

Harold. I don't know.

Maude. I suppose I did. Well, farewell, little tree. Grow
up, tall, and change, and fall to replenish the earth. Isn't
it wonderful, Harold? All around us, living things!

Harold. It's great. But they're not going to be evicted
tomorrow. Maude, I really think we should make some
plan to stop the police. I mean, I was planning a birthday
surprise for you tomorrow night.

Maude. Were you? How sweet! But you can still do
that. I don't think they'll throw me out before then.

HAROLD. But the furniture—what about that?

MAUDE. We'll eat on the floor. Besides, it will give us more room for dancing.

HAROLD. But don't you think if maybe we made a plan . . .

MAUDE. Oh, Harold, let's not talk about that. Come on, I want to show you something.

(*THEY walk Downstage and stop by a tall tree that rises up the length of the left proscenium.*)

There. How's that for a tree?

HAROLD. It's a tall one.

MAUDE. Wait till you see the view from the top.

HAROLD. You're not going to climb it, are you?

MAUDE. Certainly. I do it every time I come here. C'mon. It's an easy tree to climb. (*SHE begins to climb.*)

HAROLD. But suppose you fall?

MAUDE. I don't think about it. That's unprofitable speculation and not worth my trouble. (*SHE looks down at him.*) Are you coming yourself, or will you only hear about it secondhand?

HAROLD. (*with a sigh*) All right. (*HE begins to climb.*)

MAUDE. That's the spirit. There's a great view from the top.

HAROLD. I hope so.

(*MAUDE reaches the top and slides out on a large branch.*)

MAUDE. Oh, it's beautiful, Harold. There's a natural perch up here just for us.

(*HAROLD slides out and sits next to MAUDE. HE is keeping a firm grip on the trunk.*)

Isn't it exhilarating!

MAUDE. Yes . . . It's high.

MAUDE. Imagine! Here we are, cradled in a living giant, looking out over millions of others – and we're part of it.

HAROLD. Look! The sea. It's very windy up here.

MAUDE. Yes. We should hoist sail and strike out for the horizon. Wouldn't that be fun? I used to love sailing. Especially when we couldn't see land, and we were all alone, surrounded by the waves and the sea.

HAROLD. When was that?

MAUDE. In the twenties. I remember it was frowned upon. Considered dangerous, or unbecoming – one of those terms that the moribund use to keep the adventurous in tow. But we'll pull them along anyway, won't we, Harold? We'll hitch them to our balloon.

HAROLD. You could. But I don't know about me.

MAUDE. What do you mean?

HAROLD. Well, (*beginning to relax*) most people aren't like you. They're locked up in themselves. They live in their castles – all alone. They're like me.

MAUDE. Well, everyone lives in his own castle. But that's no reason not to lower the drawbridge and go out on visits.

HAROLD. But you agree that we live alone. And we die alone. Each in his own cell.

MAUDE. I suppose so. In a sense. That's why we have to make them as pleasant as possible – full of good books and warm fires and memories. Still, in another sense, you can always jump the wall and sleep out under the stars.

HAROLD. Maybe. But that takes courage.

MAUDE. Why?

HAROLD. Well, aren't you afraid?

MAUDE. Of what? The known I know, and the unknown I'd like to find out. Besides, I've got friends.

HAROLD. Who?

MAUDE. Humanity.

HAROLD. (*smiling*) That's a lot of friends. How do you know they're all friendly?

MAUDE. I heard a story once in the Orient about two architects who went to see the Buddha. They had run out of money on their projects and hoped the Buddha could do something about it. "Well, I'll do what I can", said the Buddha, and he went off to see their work. The first architect was building a bridge, and the Buddha was very impressed. "That's a very good bridge," he said, and he began to pray. Suddenly a great white bull appeared, carrying on its back enough gold to finish construction. "Take it," said the Buddha, "and build even more bridges." And so the first architect went away happy. The second was building a wall, and when the Buddha saw it he was equally impressed. "That's a very good wall," he said solemnly, and began to pray. Suddenly the sacred bull appeared, walked over to the second architect, and sat on him.

(*HAROLD bursts out laughing.*)

HAROLD. Awwww, Maude! You just made that up.

MAUDE. (*laughing with him*) Well, it's the truth. The world needs no more walls. What we've got to do is get out and build more bridges. (*looking round*) I should have brought my bag up. I could have done some knitting.

HAROLD. I'll go down and get it for you. (*HE starts*

down.)

MAUDE. Thank you, Harold. And bring up some nuts. I feel like something to munch. Are you hungry?

HAROLD. A little.

MAUDE. I think I have some oranges in my bag too. Wait a minute, I'll come down. (*SHE starts down. HAROLD reaches the bottom. HE looks up at the tree.*)

HAROLD. Wow! That was fun! Another new experience for me.

MAUDE. I'm glad you liked it. There's a higher one on the top of that hill over there. We could climb it and watch the sun go down.

HAROLD. All right. Anything you say. I'd climb the Matterhorn if you came with me.

MAUDE. (*SHE jumps down.*) You'd like it. It was fun.

HAROLD. (*impressed*) You've climbed it?

MAUDE. Yes. With Frederick. A long time ago. I dared him to do it. You see he had dared me to swim the Hellespont and so afterwards I had to come up with something for him. (*SHE looks in her bag.*) I don't have any oranges but how about a tangerine?

HAROLD. Thank you.

(*SHE hands him one and takes one herself. THEY sit down and begin to eat.*)

What happened to your husband?

MAUDE. He died. In the war. I never could find out just how. There was a lot of confusion after it was over and when I was able to begin looking — well, no one seemed to know.

HAROLD. You must have travelled around a lot together.

MAUDE. Oh, yes. All over the world. I remember a day like this in Shanghai. Blue sky and lots of clouds.

HAROLD. Yes, it's beautiful. So big. And so blue. To think that beyond all of that is the vast blackness of space.

MAUDE. But spreckled with uncountable stars. You know, they're shining right now – as a friend of mine used to say. We just can't see them. Just another instance she'd say of all that's going on beyond the bounds of human perception.

HAROLD. (*after a pause*) Maude, are you religious?

MAUDE. What does that mean?

HAROLD. Do you believe in God?

MAUDE. Yes! Everyone does.

HAROLD. Do they?

MAUDE. Absolutely. Deep down. It's part of being human.

HAROLD. Well then, who do you think God is?

MAUDE. He has a lot of names. Brahma, the Tao, Jove. And for the metaphysically inclined, there's The First Cause, The One Reality, or the Eternal Root. For me, I like what it says in the Koran: "God is Love."

HAROLD. (*correcting her*) It says that in *the Bible*. And anyway, it's just a cliché.

MAUDE. A cliché today is a profundity tomorrow – and vice versa. (*SHE finishes her tangerine and takes the knitting from her purse. SHE shows it to HAROLD.*) Isn't that pretty? I only learned how to do that last year.

HAROLD. But where is God? Is He inside us or outside us?

MAUDE. Both, I imagine. There is a little God inside us to show us where we've been, and a little God outside us to show us where we're going.

HAROLD. That's pretty mystical.

MAUDE. You're right, Harold . . . It's a mystery. Frankly, I'm not sure if He's Our Father or Our Mother. I only know, when I look at that tree that He is . . . very creative.

HAROLD. (*laughing HE stretches out on the grass*) This is really nice here. Makes me feel like a kid.

(*MAUDE laughs.*)

You know what I'd like to do?

MAUDE. What?

HAROLD. Somersaults.

MAUDE. Well, why don't you?

HAROLD. Naw, I'd feel stupid.

MAUDE. Come on, now, Harold. Everyone has the right to make an ass of themselves. You just can't let the world judge you too much.

HAROLD. All right. (*HE gets up and does a couple of somersaults. MAUDE applauds and HE laughs.*) Want to join me in some cartwheels?

MAUDE. No, thank you. I think I'll stand on my head.

HAROLD. What?

MAUDE. Let me put this away first. (*SHE puts her knitting away.*) And let me limber up. (*SHE does so.*)

HAROLD. Are you really going to stand on your head?

MAUDE. Watch. (*SHE kneels down, makes a triangle with her hands and kicks up – once, twice, and presto, SHE's standing on her head. HAROLD is delighted.*)

HAROLD. Wow. That is fabulous!

MAUDE. Well, it gives you a whole new perspective on things. Besides, it's very good for the circulation.

(*HAROLD kneels beside her and puts his head down like SHE did.*)

HAROLD. I'll bet you feel like you're walking the sky.

MAUDE. You mean like one of the clouds.

HAROLD. Yes. I think you'd be a wonderful cloud. Just floating around heaven all day.

MAUDE. No. Not me. I'd always want to dissolve into rain. (*SHE drops down.*) Come on, Harold, let's go watch the sun set. Oh, my hair – I must look a sight.

HAROLD. You look beautiful.

MAUDE. Oh! . . .

HAROLD. (*quietly and sweetly*) No, really. You're the most beautiful person I've ever seen.

MAUDE. Harold. (*SHE smiles.*) You make me feel like a schoolgirl.

(*HE kisses her cheek.*)

HAROLD. Thank you, for a wonderful day.

MAUDE. Wasn't it marvellous! And now we're seeing it end.

(*THEY stand up and look out at the setting sun.*)

There it goes. Sinking over the horizon where we're all going to go. The colors are changing and soon they'll be gone, leaving us in darkness . . . (*SHE smiles at him.*) and stars.

HAROLD. As your friend used to say.

MAUDE. That's right. She had faith in the stars. And that kept her going despite the cold, and the hunger, and the guards.

HAROLD. What happened to her?

MAUDE. She died in my arms. March 21, 1943 – the first day of spring. Oh, Harold, *look!*

HAROLD. What? (*HE looks out.*) It's just a seagull.

MAUDE. (*quietly*) Dreyfuss once wrote that on Devils' Island he would see the most glorious birds. Many years later in Britanny he realized they had only been seagulls. Come along, Harold, to me they will always be glorious birds.

(*THEY walk off together to watch the setting sun.*)

BLACKOUT

ACT II

Scene 4

PLACE: *MAUDE'S HOUSE.*

It is night. HAROLD and MAUDE enter the house in the dark. MAUDE turns on the overhead lights and we see that nearly all the furniture is gone and the room is in disarray. The large canopied bed has been moved in from the bedroom and left in front of the fireplace. Some of the paintings and other artifacts are missing and the impression is one of rather bleak emptiness.

HAROLD. What the heck!

MAUDE. Isn't this marvellous! It's so big and roomy.

HAROLD. Looks like a cyclone hit it.

MAUDE. Yes. I rather like a random arrangement. It shows off everything in a new light. Goodness, the bed

in the living room!—and the lamps all gone. It's like seeing everything again for the first time. (*SHE takes a
framed photograph from the mantel.*) Oh, look at this. Isn't
that pretty? (*SHE shows it to him.*)

HAROLD. What is it?

MAUDE. Oh, Harold, don't you know? It's the Coliseum
by moonlight.

HAROLD. I know that. But it's just a postcard.

MAUDE. "Just a postcard." Suppose it was the only
postcard in the world. Then everyone would flock to see
it. (*SHE takes it from him and puts it back with a smile.*)
Sergeant Doppel must have taken the plants . . . (*SHE
looks at the large nude.*) But I wonder why he didn't take
the painting?

HAROLD. (*being very practical*) Maude, what are you
going to do about tomorrow when they come back and
take the rest of this stuff away? That's what we've got
to be thinking about.

(*MAUDE is looking through the things that are left
and doesn't seem to hear him.*)

MAUDE. Maybe I'll give it to my friend, Glaucus. I think
he'd like the sculpture too. And Madame Arouet would
love the screens—what were you saying, Harold?

HAROLD. It doesn't matter, because whatever happens
I'm going to take care of you.

MAUDE. What's that?

HAROLD. You don't have to worry about a thing.

MAUDE. Oh, Harold, that's awfully sweet. I'm going to
have to think of an extra special something for you.

HAROLD. I mean it, Maude.

MAUDE. I know you do. Now why don't you make a fire

and I'll get us a little something to drink.

HAROLD. All right. (*HE begins to light the fire.*)

MAUDE. Oh, goodness – a candelabra. That's what we need. (*SHE begins to light the candles.*) Oh, my odorifics. I'll take them to the orphanage tomorrow. And those books . . . My, I have a busy day ahead of me.

HAROLD. Don't forget I'm planning a birthday surprise for you here tomorrow night.

MAUDE. Of course not, Harold. I'm absolutely thrilled. (*SHE finishes with the candles and brings them over by the bed.*) There we are. And now what we need is a little music. I think there is a Chopin concert on the radio tonight. (*SHE bangs the Chinese gong that used to be on the piano, and the room is suddenly filled with the soft music of a piano concerto. HAROLD looks around him with wonder.*)

HAROLD. That's fabulous.

MAUDE. (*nodding agreement*) Yes. Chopin, I adore. (*SHE comes over and sits on the bed.*) What a lovely fire!

HAROLD. Thank you. (*HE sits beside her.*) Those candles smell nice. What's that incense? Sandal-wood?

MAUDE. Yak Musk. But I don't think they call it that commercially. It's "Fragrance of the Himalayas", or something. "The Dali Lama's Delight." I suppose that's nicer.

HAROLD. It's more romantic.

MAUDE. Yes. I suppose it is.

(*THEY pause as THEY gaze at the fire.*)

HAROLD. Look, you can see the stars out the window.

MAUDE. Oh, yes – shining bright and clear.

HAROLD. What was that you said earlier about the stars

and your friend – the one who died.

MAUDE. She used to look up at the sky on nights like this and tell me how the light travelling from a distant star takes over a million years to reach us. In a million years, she'd say, Nature evolved the wing of a bird. So, by the time that light reaches us – who knows what will have happened. Maybe we will have evolved from a caterpillar to a butterfly, maybe we will have phased out evil, and all of us will be flying around – like angels. (*SHE pauses.*) Anyway, that was her hope . . . her faith . . . and her peace. (*MAUDE's voice trails off as SHE gazes wistfully into the fire. Suddenly SHE seems very small and fragile. HAROLD is uncertain and tongue-tied.*)

HAROLD. Maude – Maude –

(*MAUDE looks up.*)

MAUDE. Yes.

HAROLD. How about a song?

MAUDE. (*sparkling back to her old self*) Oh, what a wonderful idea, Harold.

HAROLD. (*jumping up*) I've got my banjo. I've been practicing. (*HE goes outside to get it.*)

MAUDE. But they've taken the piano away. No matter. I have a harmonica around here somewhere. We can play a duet. (*SHE opens an old box and sits on the bed.*) Look at these things . . . Goodness!

(*HAROLD comes back and takes the banjo from its case.*)

HAROLD. I've got the fingering perfectly but you'll have to help me with the tempo. I can't seem to change chords

fast enough. (*HE looks over at her, astonished.*) Maude
. . . What's the matter? You're crying.

MAUDE. I was just looking at these old things. My letters to Frederick . . . my war ration card . . . and look –
an old photograph. How different I was then – and how
much the same.

HAROLD. (*perplexed*) But, Maude . . . I've never seen
you cry before. I never thought you would. I thought you
could always be happy.

MAUDE. Harold, you are so young. What have they
taught you? Yes, I cry. I cry for you. I cry for this. I cry
at beauty – a sunset or a seagull. I cry when a man tor-
tures his brother – when he repents and begs
forgiveness – when forgiveness is refused – and when it is
granted. One laughs. One cries. Two uniquely human
traits. And the main thing in life, my dear Harold, is not
to be afraid to be human.

(*HAROLD blinks away the tears in his eyes. Reaching
out HE takes her hand in his and with the other
gently brushes the tears from her cheek. SHE
smiles slightly. Leaning forward HE kisses her
on the lips. The Chopin plays softly in the background as THEY look at each other in the candle-
light. Then taking her tenderly in his arms HE
kisses her again and as effortlessly as two raindrops
merge THEY fall back together on the canopied
bed.*)

SLOW FADE TO BLACK

ACT II

Scene 5

Place: *HAROLD'S HOUSE.*

*It is the following morning and MRS. CHASEN is
sitting in the living room talking on the telephone
with her hairdresser.*

Mrs. Chasen. No, no, Betty . . . a total failure! The
first girl fled, the second one fainted, and the third gave
me heart palpitations. What's that? . . . Oh, she was completely crazy – an actress – completely mad. She kept talking about her instrument and quoting little bits of Camille
. . . Harold? Oh, Harold was as shocked as I. But that was
Thursday afternoon. Yesterday he left in the morning to
go off somewhere and he has not yet returned . . . That's
right. He's been out all night. I don't know where he could
have been . . . No, I haven't telephoned the police. I
thought I'd first ask your advice. I mean, if he hasn't
shown up by twelve I'll have to cancel my appointment
for this afternoon . . . Oh, I know Mario will be furious,
but frankly, Betty, I don't see what else I can do . . .

*(HAROLD enters and walks across the room. MRS.
CHASEN looks up surprised to see him so non-
chalant.)*

83

. . . Betty, just a moment. (*SHE covers the phone.*) Harold
. . . where have you been?

HAROLD. I've been out all night.

MRS. CHASEN. You don't have to tell me that. I've been
a bag of nerves all morning. What I want to know is
WHERE you spent the night?

HAROLD. Mother, I'm going to get married.

MRS. CHASEN. I beg your pardon?

HAROLD. I'm going to get married. (*HE begins to walk
off.*)

MRS. CHASEN. Hold the line, Betty . . . Harold, just a
moment. You just can't walk in, say things like that and
walk out. If this is serious . . .

HAROLD. It is.

MRS. CHASEN. Then I've got to know who it is. Who
is it? Oh, don't tell me. It's the actress!

HAROLD. No.

MRS. CHASEN. Thank God! Well which is it then – the
little blonde or the mousey brunette?

HAROLD. It's neither.

MRS. CHASEN. Neither?

HAROLD. You haven't met her yet.

MRS. CHASEN. Well, who is she? What's she like?

HAROLD. Very beautiful.

MRS. CHASEN. Harold, where did you meet her?

HAROLD. In church one day.

MRS. CHASEN. Oh? Does Father Finnegan know her?

HAROLD. Yes. They're good friends. Mother, I've got
to buy an engagement ring. I'm going to propose tonight.
(*HE starts off.*)

MRS. CHASEN. Harold, wait a minute. You can't just
race into this thing. What's her background? Where's her
family from?

HAROLD. Austria. They were Austrian aristocracy.

MRS. CHASEN. (*impressed*) Socially prominent are they?

HAROLD. I think she said she was a countess.

MRS. CHASEN. A countess! Really? I wonder what that would make me.

HAROLD. Mother, I've really got to go.

MRS. CHASEN. Wait, Harold, I've got to meet her. Where does she live? I've got to make a call on the family.

HAROLD. (*exiting*) The last house on Waverly Street – number 726.

MRS. CHASEN. But, Harold, Harold – you haven't told me her name.

HAROLD. (*Offstage*) Maude.

MRS. CHASEN. Maude? . . . (*thinking it over*) . . . Maude Chasen . . . Mrs. Harold Chasen . . . (*It doesn't sound too bad to her. Suddenly SHE remembers the phone and picks it up.*) Betty? Are you there? . . . The most amazing thing has happened. Harold has found a fianceé.

BLACKOUT

ACT II

Scene 6

PLACE: *MAUDE'S HOUSE.*

The principal pieces of furniture have been removed and the place is empty except for an old trunk, and a few other odds and ends. MAUDE is tying some books together and humming merrily to herself when BERNARD enters.

MAUDE. Hello, inspector. Come right in. I've just put on the kettle. Would you care to join me in a cup of tea?

BERNARD. No, thanks.

MAUDE. But it's oat straw tea. I'll bet you've never had oat straw tea.

BERNARD. No, thanks.

MAUDE. Well, all right. But I'll never understand anyone turning down a new experience.

BERNARD. I've come from the county court. This is an eviction notice. You have twenty-four hours to leave this house.

MAUDE. Oh, that's plenty of time. I'll be gone before then. Would you put your finger over here on these books? I'm tying them up for the hospital.

(*Reluctantly HE agrees to do so.*)

BERNARD. I just want to say one more thing before I go. I suppose you think I've been hard on you . . .

MAUDE. Oh, no, inspector.

BERNARD. Well, I have. But it's nothing personal, you understand. It's just that it's my job. Someone has to keep things stable, someone has to stop people like you from rocking the boat. But I've got nothing against you personally. I wanted you to know that.

MAUDE. Oh, I know that, inspector, but how can you make life stand still? It's always changing. I mean look at this room. Last week it was full. Today it's almost empty.

BERNARD. Yes.

MAUDE. (*finishing tying the books*) There we are, thank you. Someone's coming from the hospital to pick them up. Which reminds me – I don't suppose you'd like this painting, inspector? (*SHE uncovers the large nude of herself.*) It's called "Nymphs and Shepherds Watch The Ecstasy of Saint Therese."

BERNARD. Isn't that . . . ?

MAUDE. (*coyly*) Yes.

BERNARD. No, thanks.

MAUDE. Oh, all right. Maybe I'll send it over to Father Finnegan. After all, it does have religious overtones.

(*The kettle whistles Offstage.*)

BERNARD. Goodbye, madam.

MAUDE. Goodbye, inspector. I hope we meet again.

(*MAUDE goes to the kitchen. The INSPECTOR goes outside. MRS. CHASEN, all dressed up in her finest clothes in order to meet "the countess", enters with MAUDE's address in her hand. SHE looks at MAUDE's house and is very puzzled. SHE stops the departing INSPECTOR.*)

MRS. CHASEN. Excuse me, I'm looking for the last house on Waverly Street – number 726.

BERNARD. Lady, this is the only house on Waverly Stree, and believe me one is enough. (*HE exits. MRS. CHASEN looks after him a little confused. Taking a deep breath, SHE goes and knocks on the door.*)

MAUDE. (*Offstage*) Come in.

(*MRS. CHASEN enters. MAUDE pops her head around the kitchen door.*)

Hello, the books are over there. I'm just making some

tea. Do you have time for a cup? Oh, I'm sure you do. It won't take a minute. (*SHE pops back into the kitchen.*)

MRS. CHASEN. Ah, madame . . .

MAUDE. (*Offstage*) Do you take milk or lemon? Doesn't matter. I'll bring both.

(*We can hear MAUDE humming her song in the kitchen. MRS. CHASEN resignedly looks about the room while SHE waits. After a moment MAUDE enters with a tray of tea things including an ornate silver tea pot.*)

Oh, here we are. We can sit on that trunk.

MRS. CHASEN. Excuse me, but I think I must have the wrong address.

MAUDE. Oh?

MRS. CHASEN. I'm looking for a young girl . . .

MAUDE. You're not from the hospital?

MRS. CHASEN. Eh, no.

MAUDE. (*laughing*) That's funny. I thought you were from the hospital. I'm giving them some books and they were sending someone around to pick them up.

MRS. CHASEN. Oh, I see. Well, actually I do volunteer work at the hospital from time to time but at the moment I'm looking for a young girl who is supposed to live here.

MAUDE. Really? Well, I'm the only one living here and today is my 80th birthday.

MRS. CHASEN. Eighty years old. Oh, how marvellous. Congratulations.

MAUDE. Thank you. And now you must stay for tea. (*SHE sits down and begins to pour. MRS. CHASEN is caught.*) It's been a busy day and I've still so much to do. As you can see I'm moving out and everything is all topsy-turvy. Sugar?

MRS. CHASEN. Ah, no plain, thank you. Perhaps this young girl is moving in here, do you think?

MAUDE. Could be. Here you are. Would you like a cake?

(MRS. CHASEN takes the tea and sits.)

MRS. CHASEN. No, thank you.

MAUDE. Oh, go ahead. They're almond-fig. I baked them myself.

MRS. CHASEN. Well, just one thank you.

MAUDE. You're welcome. (*SHE pours tea for herself.*)

MRS. CHASEN. Oh, that's a lovely old tea-pot.

MAUDE. Yes. It belonged to my late husband's family. Sterling silver. Do you like it?

MRS. CHASEN. Very much.

MAUDE. Let me give it to you then.

MRS. CHASEN. I beg your pardon?

MAUDE. Please. I'd love you to have it.

MRS. CHASEN. Oh, I couldn't . . .

MAUDE. Why not? I'm sure you'll take wonderful care of it.

MRS. CHASEN. Well, let me pay you for it . . .

MAUDE. Not in the least. It's yours.

MRS. CHASEN. Well, if you insist. Thank you. That's awfully sweet of you.

MAUDE. Not at all. Another cake?

MRS. CHASEN. Yes, I will. They're very tasty.

MAUDE. Take two.

MRS. CHASEN. Thank you . . . And this tea is delicious.

MAUDE. Isn't it? Oat straw.

MRS. CHASEN. Really? I'll have to get some. My friend, Betty – oh, excuse me, I haven't introduced myself. I'm

Mrs. Helen Chasen.

MAUDE. Not Harold's mother?

MRS. CHASEN. (*surprised*) Why, yes.

MAUDE. I'm so pleased to meet you. Harold has told me so much about you.

MRS. CHASEN. You're . . .

MAUDE. The Countess Mathilda Chardin.

MRS. CHASEN. The Countess? . . .

MAUDE. That's right. A silly title. You go ahead and call me Maude.

MRS. CHASEN. (*with rising intensity*) Maude . . . *Maude . . . MAUDE!*

MAUDE. Yes, Helen?

MRS. CHASEN. (*recovering*) So you know my son?

MAUDE. Oh, yes, we're great friends. He's such a wonderful boy. So intelligent and so sensitive. I love him so much. But then you know all about that, don't you?

MRS. CHASEN. Eh—yes.

MAUDE. Who's that young girl you were looking for earlier? Was that someone you wanted him to meet?

MRS. CHASEN. Not exactly.

MAUDE. I think he should get out and meet more people, don't you? I know you've tried with these computer girls (*SHE laughs.*)—Harold told me about them—but he should find someone on his own.

MRS. CHASEN. That's what I'm afraid of.

MAUDE.Well, don't be. He'll have to leave the nest sometime.

MRS. CHASEN. You said you were leaving?

MAUDE. That's right. I'll be out of here by midnight.

MRS. CHASEN. Definitely?

MAUDE. Yes. I'm off for New Horizons.

MRS. CHASEN. Then Harold hasn't told you about . . .

MAUDE. About what?

MRS. CHASEN. This is rather a delicate matter. And I'm not sure how to broach it . . . but . . .

MAUDE. Yes.

MRS. CHASEN. Did Harold ever mention marriage?

MAUDE. No. Why do you ask?

MRS. CHASEN. Well, you see he's a very impulsive boy and he has this idea . . . well, what do you think of marriage?

MAUDE. I think it's wonderful, a beautiful experience. Two people growing into one. But then, you were married and you know all about that.

MRS. CHASEN. Yes . . . but I mean what do you think of an older woman marrying a younger man?

MAUDE. I don't think it makes any difference. Do you?

MRS. CHASEN. I think to some it would.

MAUDE. Really? How about an older man marrying a younger woman?

MRS. CHASEN. That's different. That's accepted.

MAUDE. Oh I see. You're worried about what people will say.

MRS. CHASEN. Well, I mean, after all . . .

MAUDE. Has this been troubling you for a long time?

MRS. CHASEN. I just think that an older woman . . .

MAUDE. Who's been married before . . . ?

MRS. CHASEN. Yes.

MAUDE. But her husband's dead?

MRS. CHASEN. Yes.

MAUDE. And she's thinking of marrying again to a younger man?

MRS. CHASEN. Well, I . . .

MAUDE. Helen! If that's what *you* want and if that's what *he* wants, you go right ahead and marry your young man.

MRS. CHASEN. What?

MAUDE. Oh, I know some people will look down their noses – think it's odd or strange but listen to your heart and you'll never go wrong.

MRS. CHASEN. I don't think you understand. It's not me I'm worried about. It's Harold.

MAUDE. Oh, Harold will think it's marvellous. I'll talk to him if you like.

MRS. CHASEN. No. No. It's not . . .

MAUDE. Something's bothering you, isn't there, Helen? Something you want to say to me.

MRS. CHASEN. Yes, I . . .

MAUDE. It's the honeymoon, isn't it?

MRS. CHASEN. What?

MAUDE. Don't you worry about a thing. You're a fine looking woman. I'm sure there's many a cock in the barn-yard who'd like to roost on a perch with you. Believe me.

MRS. CHASEN. I think I'd better be going. (*SHE gets up. MAUDE follows her to the door.*)

MAUDE. Yes, me too. Well, it was awfully nice meeting you, Helen, and very sweet of you to confide in me. But forget that problem – with the right breathing and the right exercise you'll match him night for night.

MRS. CHASEN. Goodbye. (*SHE exits with MAUDE shouting after her.*)

MAUDE. Try standing on your head each day. It's very good for stamina and excellent for firming the bust. And . . . Oh, Helen . . . Helen . . . you forgot your teapot.

BLACKOUT

ACT II

Scene 7

Place: *THE PSYCHIATRIST'S AREA.*

*The LIGHTS COME UP immediately on the Doctor's office
    which as in Act I, Scene 2, is a small lighted area
    Downstage Right. MRS. CHASEN is discovered lying
    on the couch breathlessly spilling the story to DOCTOR
    MATTHEWS.*

Mrs. Chasen. The woman is mad, completely mad!
She's eighty, senile, and my son wants to marry her.

Doctor. Calm down, Helen. It's no use getting yourself
all worked up.

Mrs. Chasen. Worked up! I'm not worked up. I'm concerned, I'm a concerned mother!

Doctor. Yes, yes . . . perhaps we can talk to Harold,
reason with him, have it postponed.

Mrs. Chasen. I'll have it annulled!

Doctor. Helen, he's not married yet. He's not even
engaged.

Mrs. Chasen. Doctor, you don't seem to realize the
gravity of the situation. He's made up his mind. He's deter-
mined to go through with this. I know that look on his
face.

DOCTOR. All right. I'll go speak to him.

MRS. CHASEN. Tell him that a wedding is impossible. That I will never give my consent.

DOCTOR. Legally, I don't think that's required. (*HE exits.*)

MRS. CHASEN. Legally! Has a mother no rights? (*SHE crosses as the lights change to the MRS. CHASEN set. FATHER FINNEGAN enters.*) Oh, Father Finnegan, so good of you to come.

PRIEST. Not at all, Mrs. Chasen. what is it I can do for you?

MRS. CHASEN. You know my son?

PRIEST. Yes, a charming boy—very pious. I see him quite often at funerals.

MRS. CHASEN. He's going to get married.

PRIEST. Excellent news! And do I know the lucky bride?

MRS. CHASEN. The Countess.

PRIEST. The Countess?

MRS. CHASEN. Yes. Maude.

PRIEST. (*with a sudden realization*) Oh, sweet Mother of God!

(*The LIGHTS GO OUT and COME UP AGAIN on another area of MRS. CHASEN's house. HAROLD is painting letters on a large piece of canvas while HE listens to DOCTOR MATTHEWS.*)

DOCTOR. Your mother has told me about your marriage plans, Harold. She is very distraught.

HAROLD. I'm sorry to hear that.

MRS. CHASEN. (*breaking in*) Then why, Harold? Why?

DOCTOR. (*ushering her aside*) Helen, please. Let me

handle this. Now, Harold, are you sure that this planned engagement is just not another example of adolescent rebellion? After all, you did admit that your suicides were dramatic attempts to gain attention.

HAROLD. Maybe they were . . . but that's all over now. I'm throwing all that stuff away. Mother should be very happy to hear that.

MRS. CHASEN. I'm thrilled.

DOCTOR. Helen!

MRS. CHASEN. (*entering the scene*) Harold. Darling. What's come over you?

HAROLD. Love.

MRS. CHASEN. What?

HAROLD. Love. I'm in love.

MRS. CHASEN. That's not love. That's some geriatric obsession! Tell him, doctor. Tell him the woman is old enough to be his mother. Good God, she's old enough to be *my* mother!

(*FATHER FINNEGAN enters rather reluctantly.*)

PRIEST. Mrs. Chasen?

MRS. CHASEN. Oh, Father, there he is. Talk to him. Reason with him. Forbid him.

PRIEST. (*a little nervously*) Well, actually, Mrs. Chasen, I don't think I'm the right person for this affair. After all, if the boy is of age and wishes to do this . . . thing . . . I don't see where I or the Church . . .

MRS. CHASEN. (*interrupting*) But he'll listen to you. He respects you. Isn't that so, doctor?

DOCTOR. Are you all right, Father?

PRIEST. It's nothing. A little lightness in the head.

MRS. CHASEN. Oh, I know that feeling. Right now I

could collapse from anxiety. Harold, Father Finnegan
has something to say to you.

PRIEST. Eh . . .

MRS. CHASEN. (*to the PRIEST*) Tell him about the scan-
dal. Tell him about the publicity. Remember I'm depend-
ing on you. You're my final hope. (*SHE exits with the
DOCTOR. The little PRIEST approaches HAROLD.*)

PRIEST. Harold . . .

HAROLD. Yes, Father.

PRIEST. Harold . . .

HAROLD. Would you like a seat?

PRIEST. Thank you. (*HE sits opposite HAROLD.*) Well,
now . . . (*A pause. HE clears his throat. HE clears his
throat again. Finally HE begins but with each word it
is becoming more and more difficult.*) Harold, the Church,
has nothing against the union of the old and the young.
Each age has its own beauty. But a marital union is concerned with the conjugal rights. And the procreation of
children. I would be remiss in my duty if I did not tell
you that the idea of . . . (*HE swallows.*) intercourse . . .
the fact of your firm, young body . . . (*HE wipes his
forehead.*) co-mingling with the whithered flesh, sagging
breasts, and flabby buttocks of the mature female person . . . frankly and candidly . . . is one of which it can
be said that . . . I think I'm going to faint. (*HE tumbles
forward.*)

HAROLD. (*jumping up to help*) Father, what's the matter? (*calling out*) Doctor! Doctor, come here.

PRIEST. It's nothing . . . (*gasping for breath*) It's
nothing.

HAROLD. Are you all right?

PRIEST. Just a little lightness in the head. It will pass.

It will pass.

(*MRS. CHASEN and the DOCTOR enter. MRS. CHASEN stops dead.*)

MRS. CHASEN. Harold! What have you been doing to that poor little man?
HAROLD. Me? Nothing. Honestly, I didn't do anything.

(*The DOCTOR goes to the PRIEST.*)

DOCTOR. Can I help you, Father?
PRIEST. I just need some air.
DOCTOR. Here, come with me.
PRIEST. Thank you. Thank you.

(*THEY go off. MRS. CHASEN turns to HAROLD.*)

MRS. CHASEN. Oh, Harold, I don't understand it. How can you do this to me?
HAROLD. Mother, I've got to be going.
MRS. CHASEN. You're throwing your life away. Think about that. Think about what people will say.
HAROLD. I don't care what people will say.
MRS. CHASEN. You don't care! *You're* not going to have an eighty year old princess for a daughter-in-law! Oh, Harold, all I want is for you to marry a nice girl, have a nice wedding – what are you doing?
HAROLD. (*picking up the canvas*) I'm leaving.
MRS. CHASEN. You're walking out?
HAROLD. Yes.
MRS. CHASEN. But, where are you going?

HAROLD. I'm going to marry the woman I love.

MRS. CHASEN. (*quietly*) Harold. This is insane.

HAROLD. (*HE stops to look at her for a moment*) Yes. Perhaps it is. (*HE smiles and exits.*)

BLACKOUT

ACT II

Scene 8

PLACE: *MAUDE'S HOUSE.*

It is night and the stage is black. We can hear MAUDE opening the front door of her house and giggling to HAROLD.

MAUDE. Harold? Harold? Can I come in now? Oh this is so much fun. I can't see a thing.

HAROLD. Careful you don't trip.

MAUDE. What can I trip over? This place was empty this afternoon. (*SHE laughs.*) What have you been doing when I was away?

HAROLD. Da-dum! (*HAROLD suddenly turns the switch and the room is illuminated by a hundred multi-colored Christmas lights strung across the walls and around the windows. On the back wall is the large canvas banner spelling out in block letters "Happy Birthday Maude." A couple of Japanese lanterns hang from the fireplace and nearby is a large vase full of tall sunflowers. In the middle of the room is an old chair and a stool placed on either side of the trunk which is serving as a table. It is set for supper for two, complete with one lone daisy stuck in a silver vase.)*

MAUDE. (*enraptured*) This is dazzling! Whenever did you find the time?

HAROLD. Well, it took a little longer than I expected. I thought we'd make it for dinner but it looks like it will be more like a late supper.

MAUDE. It was a busy day for me too. I never did get rid of everything. You'll have to do that tomorrow.

HAROLD. I have another surprise for you tonight that I hope will take care of tomorrow.

MAUDE. Another one? Oh, Harold, I love surprises, don't you? They make me feel so . . . chiffon! Look, sunflowers!—Where did you get them?

HAROLD. I made them.

MAUDE. Really? They're beautiful.

HAROLD. But here's a real flower—from me to you. (*picking up the vase*) An individual—Remember?

MAUDE. Oh, I do. I do.

HAROLD. And now as suits the occasion . . .

MAUDE. Champagne!

HAROLD. It's all right. It's organic.

MAUDE. Harold, this is all so wonderful. It's like a hundred fireworks have exploded in this room.

HAROLD. Watch out! (*HE pops the champagne and pours two glasses.*) Well, what should we drink to?

MAUDE. You propose the toast.

HAROLD. All right. To you, Maude—yesterday—(*HE gives her the daisy.*)Today—(*HE clinks her glass.*)—and tomorrow. (*HE takes a ring box from his pocket and places it lightly on the table.*)

MAUDE. That's a perfect birthday toast.

(*THEY drink.*)

I think you're going to be a poet.

HAROLD. (*HE laughs.*) It's you who should have been the poet.

MAUDE. Me? (*SHE laughs and THEY sit.*) No, I think I should have liked to be an astronaut.

HAROLD. A what?

MAUDE. A private astronaut, able to go out and explore the unknown. Like the men who sailed with Magellan, I want to see if we really can fall off the edge of the world. What a joke it would be (*making a circle in the air*) if like them I end up where I began.

HAROLD. Like to hear a song?

MAUDE. Yes. That reminds me . . . (*SHE goes for a box.*)

HAROLD. No. Sit there. I've got my banjo. (*HE gets it.*) I've been preparing this for days . . . Ready? Here goes. (*HAROLD plays through the first verse of the song Maude taught him, making only a few hesitations and mistakes. For the second verse MAUDE stands up to sing and dance and for the final chorus HAROLD joins in the singing and together THEY build to a grand finish.*)

MAUDE. That was stupendous! You have a real feeling for music, Harold. Don't let it get away. (*SHE hands him a box.*) Here.

HAROLD. What's this?

MAUDE. A token of my affection.

HAROLD. Thank you. What is it?

MAUDE. Open it . . . and pass it on.

HAROLD. All right. But, here . . . (*HE hands her the ring box.*) Open mine first.

MAUDE. Another surprise? Oh, Harold you shouldn't

have.

HAROLD. It's a ring – not very expensive – but . . . (*with emotion*) I hope it will make you very happy.

MAUDE. Oh, I am happy. (*tenderly*) Ecstatically happy. You couldn't have given me a lovelier farewell.

HAROLD. Farewell?

MAUDE. Why yes, dear. This is my 80th birthday.

HAROLD. But you're not going anywhere, are you?

MAUDE. Yes, dear. I took the pills an hour ago. I should be gone by mignight.

HAROLD. (*HE is stupified.*) What? . . . but . . . it's . . .

(*SHE smiles at him. The realization of what SHE has
    done hits him hard.*)

Oh, my God! Quick where's the pnone?

MAUDE. The what?

HAROLD. The phone! The phone! Where's the phone?

MAUDE. I think I had one around here somewhere. I never really used it that much.

HAROLD. Well, where is it? Where's the cord?

(*HAROLD runs around the room looking for the phone.
    MAUDE joins in the search.*)

MAUDE. Maybe it's in the kitchen.

HAROLD. No, no. You sit down. You've got to conserve your strength.

MAUDE. For what?

HAROLD. Maude, *please!*

MAUDE. All right. (*SHE sits. HAROLD goes off.*) Harold, look. There's a cord running along the wall. Where does it go to?

(*HAROLD grabs the cord and pulls it off the wall. HE
    follows it across the room and out the window. HE
    opens the window and drags in the phone.*)

HAROLD. Got it. (*HE dials madly.*)
MAUDE. I knew I had one. I remember I put it out
the window because it made a lovely perch for the birds.
HAROLD. Hello, operator – get me the hospital. Quick-
ly! This is an emergency . . . Just calm yourself, Maude.
Just hold on.
MAUDE. Hold on? Hold on? (*SHE giggles.*) Oh, Harold
how absurd.
HAROLD. Hello, hospital? There's been an accident –
an overdose of drugs. Send an ambulance right away . . .
726 Waverly Street – That's right. And hurry. This is a
matter of life and death. (*He hangs up.*)
MAUDE. Oh, Harold . . .
HAROLD. No, you sit down. Just stay there and rest.
They'll be here any minute.
MAUDE. Harold, this is such a lot of fuss – So un-
necessary. Come on, give us a smile.
HAROLD. Maude . . . Please . . . (*HE kneels beside her.*)
Don't die. I couldn't bear it. Please, don't die.
MAUDE. But, Harold, we begin to die as soon as we
are born. What is so strange about death? It's no sur-
prise. It's part of life. It's change.
HAROLD. But why now?
MAUDE. I made up my mind long ago that I'd pick the
date. I thought 80 was a good number.
HAROLD. But, Maude . . .

MAUDE. Oh, I admit it's a big step to take. But you've got to have faith . . . You've got to have faith. (*SHE laughs softly.*) I feel giddy.

HAROLD. But, Maude, you don't understand. I want to marry you. Do you hear me? I love you. I've never said that to anyone in my life before. You're the first. Maude, please don't leave me.

MAUDE. Harold, don't upset yourself so.

HAROLD. It's true. I can't live without you.

MAUDE. (*Sleepily, SHE pats his head.*) "And this too shall pass away."

HAROLD. Never! Never! I'll never forget you. I wanted to marry you. I've got the ring. I was going to ask you tonight.

MAUDE. Oh, it was a lovely party, Harold. Thank you for everything.

HAROLD. Maude!

MAUDE. Farewell, Harold. (*SHE closes her eyes.*)

HAROLD. No, no, Maude, wait. Don't you understand. I love you. I love you.

MAUDE. (*smiling at him for the last time*) Oh, that's wonderful, Harold. Go – and love some more. (*SHE dies.*)

HAROLD. Maude . . . Maude?

(*The sound of the ambulance siren is approaching in the distance. HAROLD hears it get louder and louder. Through his tears:*)

Oh, Maude . . .

(*His head falls in her lap and HE begins to cry. The sirens wail louder and louder and the LIGHTS BEGIN TO*

*DIM on Maude's house. HAROLD stands up and as
if in a daze walks forward in a FOLLOW SPOT. All
around him we hear the sounds of the hospital, the
sirens, the intercom calling doctors, nurses talking,
patients being interviewed, phones ringing, etc. This
builds to a mad crescendo and is suddenly cut off.*

*The lights come up. HAROLD walks back to MAUDE's
house. MAUDE is not there but the party trappings
are exactly as we left them. Very calmly HAROLD
throws down his coat and looks around. HE goes over
to the champagne and the cake and calmly picks up
a glass. But the growing emotion in him becomes too
great and finally HE lets it explode. Throwing down
the glass, HE turns over the table, knocks down the
sunflowers, and with a terrible cry of pain pulls the
large banner off the wall. HE stops when HE sees the
little ring box. Taking it gently in his hands HE begins
to cry.)*

HAROLD. Maude . . . Oh, Maude . . .

*(With tears running down his cheeks, HE collapses on
some cushions and, sobbing hopelessly like a lost child,
HE buries his face in his arms.)*

FADE TO BLACK

LIGHTS UP:

*It is morning and the sun is shining through the windows.
HAROLD looks up awakened by the sound of birds.*

HE goes to the window, sprinkles some seeds in the catapult and pulls the release that scatters it everywhere. HE smiles in spite of himself. HE looks around the room, picks up the table, and straightens the sunflowers. HE takes the ring box and puts it in his pocket. HE picks up the banjo, but then decides to leave it. Taking his coat HE is about to exit when HE sees MAUDE's gift to him by the chair. HE sits down, opens the box and takes out the Chinese gong that used to stand on the piano. HE grins. Standing it up on the trunk HE gives it a bang. Suddenly from out of nowhere a piano begins playing the first part of the song Maude taught him. HAROLD looks about. HE can't believe it. HE has no idea where it is coming from. Suddenly it stops. Then it starts up again, playing the opening notes as if waiting for him to join in. It stops. HAROLD picks up his banjo and plays the same opening notes. The piano answers back. HAROLD smiles. HE plays the introduction; the piano joins in; and together they play with perfect coordination, virtuosity and joy . . . until

THE CURTAIN FALLS

NOTES ON STAGING BY THE AUTHOR

The most important thing to remember, I think, in staging HAROLD AND MAUDE is that the story first came to me as a screenplay and so the subsequent play, although very different from the movie, still has a feeling of cinema in its construction. The scenes are short and the action jumps from set to set. But as in a film, these jumps should be as fast and as smooth as possible so that the main thrust of the story never lags. The first way to accomplish this is in the design of the set.

The twenty scenes in this play can roughly be broken into three general categories: the small playing areas; the open space areas; and the houses for Harold and Maude. The small playing areas, for example, the psychiatrist's office, can be delineated by a circle of light and one or two pieces of furniture – in this case, a couch and a chair. Similarly, the pews and a stained glass window are enough to suggest the church. The open playing areas – the cemetery, the beach and the forest – should likewise be sketched with light and carefully selected props, but should also suggest more space, perhaps using the whole stage or even the whole theater.

The main design problem, however, is the houses for Harold and Maude. They are the two major sets and should co-exist equally. The best solution for handling this is that when one house comes on, the other disappears. In the French production directed by Jean-Louis Barrault, Maude's house was on a platform hidden upstage and was wheeled down front when needed. Harold's house was formed by flats coming in from the wings. This seemed to work well because the transitions were fast and smooth, helped by the music and the artful placement of the actors going from set to set. This plan also gave Maude's house a certain definition so that, even when emptied of all the bric-a-brac and furniture at the end of the play, it still retained its own sense of place and personality.

The other major way of keeping a cinematic flow to the play's presentation is by the use of music during the production, but particularly at the end of the scenes. In the French production, Barrault had a specific musical sting suggesting Harold's craziness that played at the close of the phony suicides; e.g., when the maid sees Harold's head on a tray, or after the computer girl's collapse. This music not only helped kick off the joke, but also helped the transition into the next set. Barrault had a similar funny musical sting for Maude at the close of some of her scenes; e.g., with the priest in the church or when she takes the priest's car for the second time.

I have indicated throughout the play where music (and sound effects, too) are to be used. Sometimes, I have even indicated specific pieces, but these should be treated as suggestions. The song that Maude teaches him could be an old one or a new one or one written specifically for the production. The only guidelines are: does it express something of what Maude is trying to teach Harold and does it work for the close of the play in bringing

Harold out of the despair of Maude's death to the joy and wonder of continuing life.

Before closing, a few words about the workings of Harold's suicide. The hanging is accomplished by a harness to support the body and a fake noose around the neck. He could carry a remote control transistor device that he could pretend was lowering him to the floor. The dynamite in the closet is done with a false back to let the actor out and then an explosion of flash powder and lots of smoke and noise. The fiery chest is done in a similar fashion. In the Barrault production one side of the chest fell down revealing a smoking skeleton. Finally, the hand chopping scene is designed to have the audience's attention fixed on the smoking rifle so that Harold can get his phony hand in place on the table without them noticing.

Two final notes: if the actress playing Maude can't whistle loud enough, an actor who can should be placed in the wings to whistle for her. If a real seal is unavailable (and I've never seen a production that has had one), a child in a seal costume is one solution; another is a large hand-puppet and, in a last resort, the seal can be played off stage.